Acting Edition

Maytag Virgin

by Audrey Cefaly

Copyright © 2017 by Audrey Cefaly
All Rights Reserved
2022 Edition

MAYTAG VIRGIN is fully protected under the copyright laws of the United States of America, the British Commonwealth, including Canada, and all member countries of the Berne Convention for the Protection of Literary and Artistic Works, the Universal Copyright Convention, and/ or the World Trade Organization conforming to the Agreement on Trade Related Aspects of Intellectual Property Rights. All rights, including professional and amateur stage productions, recitation, lecturing, public reading, motion picture, radio broadcasting, television, online/digital production, and the rights of translation into foreign languages are strictly reserved.

ISBN 978-0-573-70620-2

www.concordtheatricals.com
www.concordtheatricals.co.uk

FOR PRODUCTION INQUIRIES

United States and Canada
info@concordtheatricals.com
1-866-979-0447

United Kingdom and Europe
licensing@concordtheatricals.co.uk
020-7054-7298

Each title is subject to availability from Concord Theatricals Corp., depending upon country of performance. Please be aware that *MAYTAG VIRGIN* may not be licensed by Concord Theatricals Corp. in your territory. Professional and amateur producers should contact the nearest Concord Theatricals Corp. office or licensing partner to verify availability.

CAUTION: Professional and amateur producers are hereby warned that *MAYTAG VIRGIN* is subject to a licensing fee. The purchase, renting, lending or use of this book does not constitute a license to perform this title(s), which license must be obtained from Concord Theatricals Corp. prior to any performance. Performance of this title(s) without a license is a violation of federal law and may subject the producer and/or presenter of such performances to civil penalties. Both amateurs and professionals considering a production are strongly advised to apply to the appropriate agent before starting rehearsals, advertising, or booking a theatre. A licensing fee must be paid whether the title(s) is presented for charity or gain and whether or not admission is charged. Professional/Stock licensing fees are quoted upon application to Concord Theatricals Corp.

This work is published by Samuel French, an imprint of Concord Theatricals Corp.

No one shall make any changes in this title(s) for the purpose of production. No part of this book may be reproduced, stored in a retrieval system, scanned, uploaded, or transmitted in any form, by any means, now known or yet to be invented, including mechanical, electronic, digital, photocopying, recording, videotaping, or otherwise, without the prior written permission of the publisher. No one shall share this title(s), or any part of this title(s), through any social media or file hosting websites.

For all inquiries regarding motion picture, television, online/digital and other media rights, please contact Concord Theatricals Corp.

MUSIC AND THIRD-PARTY MATERIALS USE NOTE

Licensees are solely responsible for obtaining formal written permission from copyright owners to use copyrighted music and/or other copyrighted third-party materials (e.g., artworks, logos) in the performance of this play and are strongly cautioned to do so. If no such permission is obtained by the licensee, then the licensee must use only original music and materials that the licensee owns and controls. Licensees are solely responsible and liable for clearances of all third-party copyrighted materials, including without limitation music, and shall indemnify the copyright owners of the play(s) and their licensing agent, Concord Theatricals Corp., against any costs, expenses, losses and liabilities arising from the use of such copyrighted third-party materials by licensees. For music, please contact the appropriate music licensing authority in your territory for the rights to any incidental music.

IMPORTANT BILLING AND CREDIT REQUIREMENTS

If you have obtained performance rights to this title, please refer to your licensing agreement for important billing and credit requirements.

MAYTAG VIRGIN was first produced by Quotidian Theatre Company in Bethesda, Maryland in October of 2015. The performance was directed by Audrey Cefaly, with set design by Scott Hengen, lighting design by Don Slater and Jessie Slater, sound design by Ed Moser, costume design by Audrey Cefaly, and properties and set dressing by Heather Brooks. The Production Stage Manager was Corie Bruins. The cast was as follows:

JACK KEY. . . . . Will Hardy
ELIZABETH "LIZZY" NASH . . . . Gillian Shelly Lawler

MAYTAG VIRGIN received its southeast regional premiere at Aurora Theatre in Lawrenceville, Georgia in January of 2018. The performance was directed by Melissa Foulger, with set design by Isabel and Moriah Curley-Clay, lighting design by Kevin Frazier, costume design by Jordan Jaked Carrier, and properties design by Kathryn Muse. The cast was as follows:

JACK KEY. . . . . Brad Brinkley
ELIZABETH "LIZZY" NASH . . . . .Courtney Patterson

CHARACTERS

JACK KEY – (thirties/forties) High school physics teacher. Southern. Nearly unflappable. Even-keeled. A man of character.

ELIZABETH "LIZZY" NASH – (thirties/forties) High school English teacher. Southern. Endearingly neurotic. Strong-willed. Quick-witted and bold.

Note: Lizzy is not a busybody, nor is she a shrew, nor is she a "Karen." She is awkward and anxious and always worried she will never be enough. If she's harping on Jack it means something deeper is at play. Hint: If she's commenting on the weather, it's absolutely 100% NOT about the weather.

SETTING

The fictional town of Lenoraville, Alabama

TIME

Present day

AUTHOR'S NOTE

Our time as humans on this planet, if we want anything other than a life of complete solitude, always involves learning the hard work of love. We let go of our ideals to find some semblance of sanity. We convince ourselves that we can get by with less and that our own happiness is secondary to the task at hand. It is a great paradox. When we love fully, we lose a part of ourselves.

ACT I

Scene 1.1

(Mid-morning. August.)

(Playing Area One: Jack Key's back porch and yard, which are in total disarray, filled with moving boxes and small furniture.)

(Playing Area Two: Elizabeth Nash's back porch and yard, populated with an eclectic mix of wind chimes, bird houses, bottle trees, and folk art. There is a clothesline that runs along the edge of her property adjacent to Jack's yard, and at times like this, when it is filled with laundry [linens, tablecloths, a few aprons], it serves as a boundary [a sort of virtual "wall"] between them.)

(Playing Area Three: There is a third playing area that represents Lizzy's private dressing room, however it should not be literal and can be indicated by something as simple as a pool of light. This same area is used in Scene 2.2 when Lizzy is addressing the audience/Jesse. This space is critical, and these moments transcend naturalism. As such, resist the urge to have them played inside the confines of her home.)

(At rise: **JACK KEY** *is busy moving boxes and furniture around, in and out of the house.* **ELIZABETH "LIZZY" NASH** *emerges from her house with a pie. She approaches Jack's yard.)*

LIZZY. Hello?

JACK. *(Offstage.)* Hello?
LIZZY. *(Calling.)* Mr. Key?
JACK. *(Appearing in his doorway.)* Yes ma'am.
LIZZY. Elizabeth Nash. That's a job there, I see.

> (**JACK** *walks out onto his porch and approaches her for a handshake.*)

I'm so sorry, I've been out of town this week, I'm a bad neighbor.

JACK. Oh, alright. That's a nice place there. Good to meet ya.

LIZZY. Lizzy.

JACK. Lizzy.

> *(Regarding her colorful yard.)*

You an artist?

LIZZY. Uh…no. I mean…am I?

JACK. It's an explosion.

LIZZY. Oh. Yes, I guess so.

> *(Beat.)*

I love the color and the…well the sounds, I guess.

JACK. Aren't the bottles supposed to hang upside down?

LIZZY. Oh, yes, upside down to catch the – but I like 'em this way. They catch the rain instead of the evil spirits… I don't need any more spirits, ya know, so…

> *(Beat.)*

When they get too full, they don't sing real well, so I do have to patrol now and then, and, uh…feed the weeds or whatever.

> *(Beat.)*

Well. Neighbors. Am I keeping you from –

JACK.	**LIZZY.**
No, no, it's –	I can come back.

JACK. It's fine. It's fine.

LIZZY. Okay. Well, welcome to the neighborhood.

JACK. Alright.

LIZZY. And to the city too, teaching over at the high school, have I got that right?

JACK. That's right.

LIZZY. Up from Biloxi?

JACK. You seem to have the advantage.

LIZZY. Oh, I hope that's alright if I take an interest in my new neighbor. I guess the days of welcome wagons are all over, but I just had to bring you a pie or something.

(Beat.)

Or maybe you don't eat pie, are you a diabetic?

JACK. I eat pie, yes ma'am I do.

LIZZY. *(Nervously.)* It's really nothing. I mean it is a pie, but it's – I could bake one in my sleep.

JACK. Very sweet of you.

(She holds on to the pie, as if carrying a security blanket.)

LIZZY. *(Regarding the house.)* How do you like it?

JACK. It's a keeper.

LIZZY. Isn't it great?

*(**LIZZY** turns to look up at the house, shielding her eyes from the sun, straining the buttons on her blouse. **JACK** notices…)*

JACK. Yes, it is.

LIZZY. It's got good bones.

JACK. Mmm hmm.

LIZZY. You think you can do something with it?

(Beat.)

JACK. Mmm hmm…

LIZZY. Well good! I was so happy to hear somebody had bought the place. Not exactly a selling point: *dead man's house*.

JACK. I'm aware of the story.

LIZZY. Oh good. See any ghosts yet?

JACK. Not a one.

LIZZY. Well, that's good. I mean they were lovely people, but you never know about a ghost.

(Beat.)

That sounds like I know something about ghosts, I have nothing to base that on, really.

(Beat.)

LIZZY. Oh my gosh, I just thought of something, did you take the front room?

JACK. The front room?

LIZZY. For the master, I mean?

JACK. Uh…yeah.

LIZZY. Oh…

(Beat.)

Well, that's where he died. Mr. McElway…

JACK. In the front room?

*(**LIZZY** gives him a pained expression.)*

I did not know that.

LIZZY. *(Almost a whisper.)* Yes, and his wife Minnie Faye a few months before.

JACK. Oh.

LIZZY. *(Horrified.)* Oh, lord, Mr. Morgan didn't tell you?

JACK.	**LIZZY.**
I don't –	What good is a realtor – I'm gon' get him. I should have been here to tell you!
No, no…I, uh…	I am so sorry.

JACK. *(Unsettled.)* You wanna sit down?

LIZZY. *(Concerned.)* Do you?

JACK. *(Exiting into the house.)* Excuse me…

LIZZY. Alright…

> (JACK *exits into the house, leaving* LIZZY *alone on the porch, unsure if he plans on returning.*)

(Calling.) Well that was thoughtless of me. I mean sometimes you say things, they need to be said, but maybe just not…

> *(To herself.)*

…not like that. Stupid Lizzy.

> *(Calling.)*

I'm so sorry. I guess I figured you knew the whole story…you said you knew the…story. Not that I believe in ghosts, but you just never know about the hereafter. If you start seeing dead people you might wanna – well, I don't know what you'd do about that, but let's just hope you don't.

> *(Beat.)*

It's a beautiful day for…construction. I really am sorry I wasn't here to help you move in, Mr. Key. I've been up at my brother's in Savannah –

> (JACK *re-enters the porch, wiping his face with a tea towel and handing* LIZZY *a cold Coca-Cola.*)

Oh, thank you.

JACK. Lemme get this…

LIZZY. Mr. Key, are you alright?

> (JACK *rather abruptly begins moving boxes out of her way.*)

Oh, don't fuss.

> *(Beat.)*

Do you need me / to –

JACK. Nope.

LIZZY. *(Almost overlapping.)* Alright.

> *(Beat.)*

You know, I'm a teacher there too. At the high school.

> *(Beat.)*

LIZZY. I'm on a leave of absence.

JACK. I'm sorry for that. I heard about your husband.

LIZZY. What have you heard?

JACK. An accident. He fell?

>   (**LIZZY** *nods.*)

It was recent?

LIZZY. We buried him a month ago, Sunday.

JACK. Awful thing.

>   (**JACK** *leans against the porch railing, drinking his Coke as* **LIZZY** *drinks hers. Neither notices the awkward silence, each in their own memory.*)

LIZZY. Sometimes I feel like I have a scarlet "W" on my chest, the way people talk and stare. It's like you're branded. You ever notice when people come up to you and they hadn't seen you in a while, and no matter how long it's been, they take that tone with you, you know the one people use when someone has died?

>   (*Beat.*)

In this case, I mean, someone *has* died, but they still take that *tone* with you – *I'm so sorry…someone has died.* As if that's the only allowable tone. I mean there must be some other tones out there, but that's the one, you know, they use, or whatever.

JACK. You say it all out loud, huh?

LIZZY. (*Mortified.*) I've brought nothing but death into your yard. Mr. Key, I am so sorry, I don't know your situation.

>   (*Beat.*)

Do you need some help unpacking?

JACK. I can manage.

LIZZY. Alright.

JACK. Thank you.

LIZZY. You just let me know what you need, I may not be able to lift the heavy stuff, but I know all the high school boys and I can make the sandwiches.

>   (**JACK** *smiles politely.*)

Have you met Mr. Sutherland? In the Cape Cod?

JACK. Ah, yes, I have.

LIZZY. He is the sweetest neighbor.

JACK. Real nice.

LIZZY. He can fix wiring, too. And he doesn't charge anything. His family has money and he just does it to pass the time in his golden years. But they left you in good shape, it's a good house and you won't have any trouble. Most likely you won't.

JACK. I like a challenge.

LIZZY. When I saw you leaning against that porch railing just now, I thought you reminded me of him. Mr. McElway, I mean. He never could sit still, especially after Miss Minnie Faye died. Oh that was a terrible thing, we all felt that one.

>   (*Beat.*)

So you teach physics?

JACK. There's a lot you know.

LIZZY. I know nothing about physics.

JACK. I don't know much myself.

LIZZY. Oh, I don't believe that. I teach English.

JACK. Yes I know. I'm in your room. 202.

LIZZY. 202? What'd they do, put you in there?

JACK. I don't know.

LIZZY. Who's in 308?

JACK. Uh…

>   (**LIZZY** *walks through Jack's yard, looking at the mess.*)

LIZZY. *(Rapid-fire.)* Three-oh-four, three-oh-six, three-oh-eight: math, math, physics on three; English, history, civics on two. There must be something goin' on up on three –

(**LIZZY** *notices a small statue of the Virgin Mary on Jack's porch.*)

LIZZY. Is that the Virgin Mary?

JACK. Yeah…

LIZZY. Hmm.

(**LIZZY** *looks around suspiciously.*)

JACK. Actually now that I think about it, I believe they are doing some painting up on the floor above me.

LIZZY. *(Distracted.)* How's that?

JACK. I think I've seen some workers in and out.

LIZZY. Ooooh, have they started that, okay, that makes more sense now.

JACK. Probably just a temporary situation.

LIZZY. I imagine.

JACK. I guess I won't unpack then.

LIZZY. Unpack. Why not?

JACK. At the school.

LIZZY. Oh, at the school.

JACK. In case they plan on moving me.

LIZZY. To 308.

JACK. 308, right.

LIZZY. That building could be hit by a hurricane, they'd prop it up with sticks. I don't know what it's gon' take to get a new school in this district.

JACK. It's quite an old building, yes ma'am.

(*Beat.*)

LIZZY. *(Pointedly.)* We can leave off the ma'am.

JACK. Alright…

LIZZY. It's not dried up and dead or anything.

JACK. No…

LIZZY. Still has some life in it.

(*Moving on now.*)

We need a proper school, Mr. Key. One with lab equipment and decent plumbing, wouldn't you agree?

JACK. I believe I would.

LIZZY. So many desperate people here, Mr. Key. Desperate, desperate people. No jobs, there's nothing here. Tired old men, hard labor up in their seventies over at the mill or on a rooftop or crawling under houses on a Sunday. Mr. McElway was installing new urinals over at the truck stop three days before he passed away. So undignified.

JACK. My daddy was a trucker until he was seventy-seven. I never saw the man.

LIZZY. How sad.

JACK. I never knew anything different.

LIZZY. But your mama must have hated that.

JACK. I don't know. She had her card games. Bingo. Always in the garden. With a cigarette.

LIZZY. She sounds like someone I wanna know.

JACK. You want another Coke?

LIZZY. Oh, no, I'm fine.

(Beat.)

How is 202, Mr. Key?

JACK. It's alright.

LIZZY. Is it a mess? Did I leave a mess?

JACK.	**LIZZY.**
No, no, it's –	If my things are in the way, I can –

JACK. They're not in the way.

(Beat.)

LIZZY. Ten years in that room.

JACK. Long time.

LIZZY. Full of secrets, 202.

JACK. Secrets?

LIZZY. Secrets.

JACK. Like what?

LIZZY. *(Playfully.)* Do you know what a secret is? Oh, I bet you do. I bet you know your way around a secret. In fact, I bet you know the secret of all secrets. The inner workings of a secret. There must be some law, some axiom of secrets in the / scientific community – some algorithm –

JACK. *(Amused, but "over it.")* Are you done?

LIZZY. You'll get used to me.

JACK. Oh, I don't wanna do that.

LIZZY. I'm a menace.

JACK. Something…

LIZZY. *(In a fake panic.)* Run! Run for your life! Oh, that's right, you can't, you have a mortgage!

JACK. Too late.

LIZZY. Tragic situation.

JACK. I see that now. *(Playfully.)* Buyer's remorse.

LIZZY. *(Charmed as hell.)* Buyer's remorse, yes, yes, absolutely!

(Awkward pause.)

What time is it, I better get to my laundry.

JACK. You don't have a dryer?

LIZZY. Do you know, I never have?

JACK. What?

LIZZY. I've never used one. Never had the need to.

JACK. You've *never* used a dryer?

LIZZY. I – it's – trust issues.

*(**LIZZY** begins taking clothes off the line.)*

JACK. *(Amused.)* What's to trust about a dryer, you trust it'll actually dry your clothes?

LIZZY. Mind your business.

*(**JACK** exits into the house.)*

(Calling.) That was a joke.

JACK. *(From offstage.)* One sec.

LIZZY. *(Calling.)* So, are you like a real Catholic or one of those cafeteria Catholics?

JACK. *(From offstage.)* A real Catholic?

LIZZY. *(Calling.)* You have a statue.

JACK. *(From offstage.)* Religion is a touchy subject.

LIZZY. *(Calling.)* Yes it is.

JACK. *(From offstage.)* Might be better discussed over dinner than a picket fence.

>　*(Beat.)*

LIZZY. *(Calling.)* You don't have a fence.

>　(**JACK** *re-enters with an old, military-style canvas rucksack.*)

JACK. That was a metaphor.

LIZZY. I know what it was.

JACK. You don't miss much.

LIZZY. What is that?

JACK. It was in the crawl space…above the porch.

LIZZY. Is this his?

JACK. I don't know.

LIZZY. It's so old…doesn't it look old to you?

JACK. It does.

LIZZY. He doesn't have any family, not that I know of. He outlived all of 'em.

>　(**LIZZY** *opens the bag.*)

Mr. Key. Did you see all this?

JACK. No, what is it?

LIZZY. Oh my gosh, letters? Letters maybe? My goodness. So many…there must be hundreds. This one looks old, is this a – it's a love letter. From Mick.

>　*(Amused.)*

Mick and Minnie.

>　(**LIZZY** *reads a few lines.*)

Oh, this is personal.

(She quickly puts the letters away.)

LIZZY. This feels wrong.

JACK. You want me to put it back?

LIZZY. *(Suddenly territorial.)* No!

> *(Beat.)*

No, I'll think about what to do.

JACK. Alright.

LIZZY. I'll look through it.

> *(She goes to leave with the rucksack and the pie.)*

You let me know if you need some moving help.

JACK. You can leave the pie, but I don't mind chasin' you for it.

LIZZY. Lost my head.

> **(LIZZY** *returns with the pie and hands it to* **JACK.** *She collects her laundry basket and walks to her porch.)*

JACK. Miss Maymee Fuller came by with some cookies last night.

LIZZY. Is that right?

JACK. She seems nice.

LIZZY. Maymee Fuller cooks with arsenic. Oh…and there are weevils in her pantry.

JACK. Damn. What'd she do to you?

LIZZY. *(She exits.)* Welcome to the neighborhood!

> **(JACK** *exits into his house with the pie, screen door slamming.)*
>
> *(Lights fade.)*

Scene 1.2

(Lights up to reveal Jack's yard, more cluttered than before. There is now a Maytag dryer visible on his porch.)

(LIZZY emerges onto her porch with a laundry basket and another pie. She deposits the laundry basket near the clothesline and walks into Jack's yard just in time to see a box being hurled out of his back door.)

LIZZY. *(Calling.)* How are you Mr. Key?

JACK. *(Appearing in his doorway.)* Hey there.

LIZZY. I can't wait till this heat breaks, can you? It's a bit too warm for September.

> *(Beat.)*

So what's with the porch, Mr. Key? Is that a Maytag? It's been out here a while…

JACK. Okay.

LIZZY. *(Smiling sweetly.)* Can I help you move it? Please?

> *(Handing him the pie.)*

It's tomato, red onion and cheddar. Eat it before I do.

JACK. *(Looking over the pie.)* Man…

LIZZY. Sometimes I make it with hot peppers too, but I didn't know your taste.

JACK. Oh, I like the heat.

LIZZY. It's just whatever I have in my garden.

JACK. Thank you.

> *(**JACK** exits into his house with the pie.)*

LIZZY. *(Calling.)* That there is my mama's recipe. You have to use the heirloom tomatoes, or don't bother.

JACK. *(From offstage.)* You tryin' to fatten me up or what?

> *(**LIZZY** looks around at the mess.)*

LIZZY. *(Under her breath.)* Guess it's true what they say about progress…

(Calling.)

LIZZY. Mr. Key, are you movin' in or movin' out?

JACK. *(From offstage.)* How's that?

LIZZY. *(Calling.)* What is all this?

JACK. *(Emerging from the house.)* Oh, I'm just doing some rearranging.

LIZZY. Rearranging?

JACK. Remodeling.

LIZZY. Well, which is it, rearranging or remodeling?

JACK. Would you like a Coke?

LIZZY. Yes, while you answer my question.

(JACK reaches into the cooler on his porch to get her a drink.)

JACK. I just noticed some things that need doing here and there.

LIZZY. Like what?

JACK. Oh, you know, painting, plastering, other things.

LIZZY. Other things…

(LIZZY looks around a bit more. She notices a beautiful wind chime on Jack's porch. She touches it, smiling.)

I've always loved this house.

(He hands her a Coke.)

Mr. Key…have you been sleeping out here?

(Beat.)

You can answer but I already know the answer. Mr. McElway used to sleep out here when he and Miss Minnie Faye would squabble and they would get so loud, they would rattle the house. You know sometimes, I don't know if you noticed, you can hear across the yard there to things goin' on at the other house.

(Beat.)

JACK. I hadn't noticed.

LIZZY. Well, anyway, I told him he needed a sleeping porch, you know, with some netting or curtains or somethin' to keep out the bugs and whatnot. Might be a good idea. I've thought about doin' that at my place.

JACK. You got the room for it.

LIZZY. Maybe.

JACK. I could help you out with that.

LIZZY. Oh, you wanna help me with my sleeping porch?

JACK. Sounds like a weekend.

LIZZY. *(Nervously.)* You keep your lawn so nice.

JACK. Just busy work.

LIZZY. Oh, I know all about that. Anything to keep the dark thoughts away. Richard Bandler, do you know him? He has a meditation for clearing out those negative thoughts. It's not very ladylike, but I do it, I do.

> *(**LIZZY** sits upright, closes her eyes, inhales deeply, and exhales the mantra:)*

Shutthefuckupshutthefuckupshutthefuckupshutthefuckup…

JACK. *(Highly amused.)* Does it work?

LIZZY. Yep! I do a lot of cooking too. But then there's no one around to eat it, so…

> *(Beat.)*

The problem is the grocery store. I'm only one person, I do not need that much asparagus. But it's not like you can divide up the package: "No, I'm cooking for one."

JACK. You can cook for me.

> *(Beat.)*

LIZZY. *(Blushing.)* I cooked for Mr. McElway just about every day after Miss Minnie Faye died. We got real close there toward the end. That sweet man. I think he knew something wasn't right about me and Jesse, but he was too afraid to ask, ya know. He would say things like, "You're a good woman, Lizzy…you go and get happy." And then he died of a broken heart. Is there a worse way to die?

(Beat.)

LIZZY. Oh, my gosh, the letters. I didn't tell you about the letters.

(LIZZY goes to her laundry basket and pulls out a small stack of letters.)

I went to see the estate lawyer. He took one look at 'em and sent me home. There's no one. Just you and me.

JACK. Have you read 'em?

LIZZY. Mr. Key, I can't tell you, it's like a puzzle. I got 'em all spread out on my kitchen table, tryin' to make sense of it. Like, these…quite obviously from when he was in the war. And these…these from when she went up to Montgomery for something like a year, I think, to see about her sister back in '96, I remember Miss Alice was going through the chemo. But some of these, I can't make it out…it's like the handwriting of a child…

JACK. *(Looking at the letters.)* Oh, wow…

LIZZY. And these…these have never been opened. Five letters.

JACK. They look recent.

LIZZY. Yeah.

JACK. You gon' read 'em?

(Beat.)

Maybe start with the oldest ones?

LIZZY. Oh, that's a good idea! Okay.

(LIZZY puts the letters back in the laundry basket.)

Kinda creepy isn't it? Readin' through other people's letters. It's like lookin' through somebody's underwear drawer.

(LIZZY begins sorting out her laundry [washcloths, bath towels, hand towels, tea towels] and hanging clothes on the line. JACK watches her a moment. He reaches into the cooler for an apple.)

JACK. So, when you comin' back to work?

LIZZY. Don't ask me that.

JACK. You been out a little bit.

LIZZY. *(Thinking.)* Three months. *Three months?* Wow…

>   (**JACK** *walks over to Lizzy's clothesline and watches her hang laundry as he eats his apple.*)

JACK. You do a lotta laundry.

LIZZY. I do. It's my addiction, I can't explain, it's like yoga.

JACK. You know, there's a dryer. Right here, on my back porch. You're more than welcome.

LIZZY. I'm not going to use your dryer, Mr. Key.

JACK. You don't like my Maytag?

LIZZY. I'd like it off the back porch.

JACK. Heated steam cycle.

LIZZY. Heated steam cycle? That's a selling point?

JACK. Wrinkle guard…

LIZZY. I have been doing my laundry the same way since grade school, Mr. Key. I do not need a dryer, I will never need a dryer.

JACK. You're not the least bit curious?

LIZZY. *(Changing the subject.)* You still in 202?

JACK. Oh, they moved me up.

LIZZY. Oh, yeah?

JACK. Yep. Up on three now.

LIZZY. Oh, okay. Fresh coat of paint?

JACK. New lights. New paint. It's nice.

LIZZY. Well, good.

>   *(Beat.)*

Do they ask about me?

JACK. Yeah.

LIZZY. What do they say?

JACK. Umm…it's a mix…

LIZZY. Okay. *Good.*

>   *(Off* **JACK***'s smile.)*

You have a nice smile, Mr. Key.

(Beat.)

JACK. Bob Searcy *[pronounced: "Sir-see"].*

LIZZY. *(Alarmed.)* Don't say it.

JACK. He is sweet…on…you.

LIZZY. Stop. Stop. Stop!

JACK. You don't like him?

(Beat.)

LIZZY. Mr. Key…have you not noticed his halitosis problem?

JACK. Halitosis?

LIZZY. Do not encourage him!

JACK. Oh, I think I need to.

LIZZY. Mr. Key!

JACK. Lots and lots.

(Beat.)

*(**LIZZY** glares at him.)*

LIZZY. *(Slow and deliberate.)* I will create such pain in your world, you will pray for the sweet release of death.

*(**JACK** bites into his apple.)*

JACK. *(Mouth full.)* You keep making promises.

LIZZY. Let's talk about *real* life, how 'bout that? *Actual* things. What else have you been up to, you makin' friends?

JACK. Umm…I got up to Montgomery last week.

LIZZY. Oh yeah?

JACK. Went on a date.

LIZZY. Uh oh!

JACK. It was so awful.

LIZZY. Oh no.

JACK. That girl would not stop talkin'. I took her over to Old Cloverdale for a bite, you ever eat over at Sinclair's?

LIZZY. Fried tomatoes…

JACK. Shrimp and grits.

LIZZY. I die!

JACK. I know!

LIZZY. So what happened?

JACK. She was just tellin' me her life story.

LIZZY. Oh, Lord.

JACK. She wore me out.

LIZZY. You do a lot of dating?

JACK. I don't. It was just a setup, blind date kinda thing.

LIZZY. Oh, I hate that.

JACK. I don't think I'll do that again.

LIZZY. I wouldn't know the first thing about datin'.

JACK. So painful. It's not what I remember. People don't *engage* anymore, you notice that?

LIZZY. How do you mean?

JACK. Well, everything is a damn text message. I'd rather just know a woman. Face to face.

LIZZY. Did you kiss her?

(Off **JACK**'s *non-verbal "no.")*

Why not?

JACK. *(Thinking.)* I didn't feel it.

LIZZY. I'm being nosy.

JACK. *(In agreement.)* Yeah.

LIZZY. Did she want to be kissed?

JACK. Yes.

LIZZY. How do you know?

JACK. She told me.

LIZZY. She *told* you?

JACK. Well, not in words, no…

LIZZY. How?

JACK. It was obvious.

LIZZY. Obvious?

JACK. Yeah…in her eyes.

LIZZY. But you didn't want to?

JACK. Naw, ya know, I just didn't want to.

LIZZY. Is she pretty?

JACK. She is…but you know, there's more to a woman than that.

LIZZY. Oh, *whatever!*

JACK. I kiss who I want to.

LIZZY. *(Playfully.)* You just go around kissing people?

JACK. *(Amused.)* Yeah, that's what I meant.

LIZZY. You gon' see her again?

JACK. No.

LIZZY. Why not?

JACK. I told you, she talks too much.

LIZZY. Well, maybe she was nervous.

JACK. *I* was nervous. I was quiet.

LIZZY. Well, maybe if you were so quiet, that's why she was so nervous, ever think o' that?

JACK. I was *listenin'*.

LIZZY. Well, don't be so selfish!

JACK. I thought you said you didn't know anything about datin'.

LIZZY. It doesn't matter anyway, she's through with you.

JACK. Oh really?

LIZZY. Yep.

JACK. And how do you know that?

LIZZY. Because if she wanted that kiss the way you say she did, and you didn't give it to her, then she's probably mortified and never wants to speak to you again.

JACK. Mortified?

> (**JACK** *pulls out his phone. He opens the text messages from Daphne, hands the phone to* **LIZZY**.)

LIZZY. *Daphne?* That's her name, Daphne? Is that her picture? I can't click it, make it bigger.

> *(He takes the phone and enlarges the picture. Hands the phone back.)*

Oh, she's cute. Some people are so cute. How do I get it back?

JACK. What do you want?

LIZZY. I want the part where she's mortified.

>(**JACK** *assists with the phone.* **LIZZY** *reads.*)

"Thank you for a lovely evening. I cannot wait to see you again."

JACK. Mortified.

LIZZY. What kind of an idiot sends a message like that when she knows you didn't wanna kiss her?

JACK. I don't think she knew that. Maybe I was just being polite.

LIZZY. That is a really good point, and you know that is what is wrong with you boys, you all are just too complicated.

>*(Beat.)*

She sent you all these pictures? She takes too many selfies.

>*(Beat.)*

You didn't reply.

JACK. Yes, I did.

LIZZY. *(Holding up the phone.)* No, you didn't.

JACK. I *called* her.

LIZZY. *(Confused.)* Called her?

JACK. *(Pointing to the phone.)* On the phone!

LIZZY. Oh. Well, what'd you tell her?

JACK. You are something else.

>*(Beat.)*

She knows I won't be calling again, let's just put it that way.

LIZZY. What's the real reason?

JACK. For what?

LIZZY. For why you didn't kiss her?

>*(Beat.)*

How long has it been?

JACK. You like to ask a personal question.

(Beat.)

JACK. You first.

LIZZY. Nuh uh…

JACK. No deal.

LIZZY. You have to call her back.

JACK. Who?

LIZZY. Is there some *other* Daphne? You need to take a step.

JACK. Oh, do I?

LIZZY. Is that some crazy notion?

JACK. I went on the date!

LIZZY. Blind date. Doesn't count.

JACK. Man alive!

   (LIZZY turns to exit with her laundry basket.)

LIZZY. *(Calling.)* Coercion, forced. It's a good thing you're not *my* type.

JACK. Oh, I'm not your type?

   (LIZZY howls with laughter.)

LIZZY. No!!

   (LIZZY exits into her house.)

JACK. *(Calling.)* So funny!

   (To himself.)

Hilarious.

   (JACK exits into his house.)
   (Lights fade.)

Scene 1.3

(Lights up to the sound of a lawn mower, which runs for a few moments and then stops. **LIZZY** *sits on her porch stoop, surrounded by letters.)*

LIZZY. *(Reading.)* "In the early days, they told us to travel light. But the worry is the heaviest of all. You looked so pretty in that velvet dress. It was all I could do not to –

*(***LIZZY*** blushes and looks around to see if anyone is watching.)*

It was all I could do not to take you up in my arms and cover you with kisses –

*(***LIZZY*** looks up to see* **JACK** *entering his yard, covered in sweat and dirt. He goes to his porch, removes his gloves, and pulls a bottle of water out of his cooler. She returns to reading the letter, but is now somewhat distracted.)*

I wanted to hold you until my arms fell off from the holding, and I wouldn't need my arms anyway, if you were my girl...

*(***LIZZY*** looks up to see* **JACK** *pouring water on his face and shoulders. She tries desperately to keep focus on the letter...)*

You don't know the effect you have on me, Miss Minnie Faye –"

*(***JACK*** removes his t-shirt.)*

(To herself.)

That...is NOT happening.

*(***JACK*** wipes his face and chest with the t-shirt.)*

(Reading, somewhat furiously now.)

"Please think about what I asked you. I'm a wreck. And I know I will be until I can see your sweet face again. Wait for me. Will you?"

(JACK *grabs a beer from the cooler and exits into the house, screen door slamming. The sound of the door jolts* LIZZY. *She stands abruptly and turns to exit, spinning back around almost instantly to retrieve the letters she nearly left behind.*)

(Flustered.)

LIZZY. Shit.

(She looks over at Jack's house.)

SHIT!

(She exits.)

(Lights fade.)

Scene 1.4

(Early December. Late afternoon. More clutter than ever in Jack's yard. Lizzy's clothesline is filled with a load of whites [sheets and a few delicates, including a full-length slip and a silk robe].)

*(Throughout the following scene, as **LIZZY** orbits all around him, **JACK** climbs up and down a ladder, hanging a strand of Christmas lights on his porch. [Note: **JACK**, nearly unflappable, stays patient and calm. He remains focused on the intricate task of light-hanging, rarely stopping to look directly at Lizzy.])*

*(**LIZZY** emerges from her house with an empty laundry basket and walks over to Jack's yard.)*

LIZZY. HAVE YOU LOST YOUR MIND?!

JACK. Lizzy.

LIZZY. You have installed a graven statue of Mary at the end of your driveway, do you want to go to hell?!

JACK. That's a pretty dress.

LIZZY. You don't even know what you've done, do you? You need to get down here. God does not share his glory with another, not even Jesus' mama, first commandment!

JACK. You know the trouble with Protestants is, they don't know how to think for themselves.

LIZZY. That is not a very Christian thing to say.

JACK. Well now, correct me here, but I believe you have a Virgin Mary in your yard too, right there by the manger.

LIZZY. What? Oh, be serious.

JACK. Well don't you?

LIZZY. Yes, Mr. Key! I do, but she's not the focus!

JACK. Oh, okay.

LIZZY. She's a *supporting character*. In a Christmas Nativity!

JACK. Oh, I see. So Jesus is the focus.

LIZZY. That's right. Jesus is the focus.

JACK. Like the flashing baby Jesus…

LIZZY. The what?

JACK. Over in Zeke's yard. He has a flashing baby Jesus.

> *(Beat.)*

Not like *flashing*, no, like *blinking*, on and off.

LIZZY. Oh, flashing…

JACK. You haven't seen it?

LIZZY. I have not.

JACK. Like some neon sign at a cheap motel: *Born today. Born today.*

LIZZY. That sounds perfectly festive and seasonally appropriate.

JACK. Why don't you take a walk down there and then we'll talk.

LIZZY. No, I don't need to take a walk, I know all I need to know right here and you really should be focusing on your own yard and the fact that your Maytag dryer is still on the porch.

JACK. You are somethin' else.

LIZZY. Mr. Key.

JACK. Why do I care what anybody sees from my side yard?

LIZZY. Oh, you are not foolin' anybody, I can see your house of horrors from my kitchen window, Mr. Key. And so can all the other neighbors up that way, and anybody who drives by from Oak Street. It seems to me, you spend hours and hours with your crisscross patterns and gardening scissors like it's the eighteenth hole at Cambrian Ridge, / and yet you can't be bothered to move the –

JACK. Bill Stanley has two rusted-out Mustangs in his back forty and another one on blocks. It's been there since June. I actually care about my property, Lizzy. You wanna come back when you have something serious to complain about?

LIZZY. Appliances belong inside, Mr. Key.

JACK. I'm not moving my dryer, Lizzy.

LIZZY. Is there a storage problem?

>*(Beat.)*

Mr. Key?

>*(Beat.)*

…Or some overarching reason why you need to have it outside in plain view?

>*(Beat.)*

What is the big deal? Just move it inside and plug it in.

>*(Softening.)*

Please…I'm trying to understand.

JACK. Well, if you must know…oddly enough, I find it comforting.

LIZZY. What? Oddly comforting.

JACK. *(Pointing to a box of nails.)* Hand me that, would ya?

LIZZY. Mr. Key, am I to understand that you mean for this to be a permanent arrangement?

JACK. *(Regarding the nails.)* I got it.

>*(**JACK** descends the ladder to fetch the nails.)*

LIZZY. Mr. McElway is pitching a fit in his grave! Are you serious? You cannot be serious.

>*(Beat.)*

Mr. Key! You know folks have been airing their laundry outside for quite some time, or maybe you've never heard of such a thing called a clothesline?

JACK. Lizzy, I don't dictate what you put on your porch.

>*(**JACK** pulls the strand of lights across a section of the porch, briefly entangling **LIZZY** in the wires.)*

LIZZY. *(Batting at the wires.)* No…no! I'm not talking about variations on taste and decor, Mr. Key. Please don't try to warp the subject.

>*(Beat.)*

And you do have a bed, right? Inside the house? What is goin' on out here, do you ever go inside?

JACK. I go in there to cook.

LIZZY. Good Lord, this is not the sticks, okay, where people burn trash and run on septic, Mr. Key…

JACK.

We are on Ft. Dale Road, a very desirable address.

You sound like a horrible person, right now…

And I assure you that I speak for all of us…

Bossy.

LIZZY. …When I tell you that we do not find it oddly comforting, not at ALL comforting. We just find it odd!

    (Beat.)

JACK. You really know how to hurt a man.

LIZZY. Mr. Key.

JACK. Cut deep, Lizzy.

LIZZY. Oh, stop it!

JACK. There are worse things than being odd, girl. I like oddness, I like it a lot. You need to loosen up.

LIZZY. Don't. You. Dare…

JACK. No, I mean it. It's a fine thing for you to go around telling people all day how it should be. Now when do you rest, I wonder?

LIZZY. *(Prideful.)* I don't sleep, I never sleep.

JACK. That's a problem.

LIZZY. Off. Topic.

JACK. I think you need to put your laundry away and get a life. This ain't healthy what you do.

LIZZY. Excuse me?

    (Beat.)

    (JACK *looks down at* **LIZZY.)**

JACK. You are such a beautiful woman, you know that?

LIZZY. I am about to knock. Your. Head off!

JACK. *(Repositioning the ladder.)* Looking forward to it.

LIZZY. I want your word that you will move that dryer.

JACK. I cannot give you that.

LIZZY. I do not want to have to take further action.

JACK. Come on over and have dinner with me.

>   *(Beat.)*

LIZZY. *(Stunned but determined to stay on topic.)* It would be embarrassing for all of us.

JACK. Homemade ginger beer. Steak.

LIZZY. You are putting me in a very uncomfortable position!

JACK. We can hang out on the porch and talk like real people.

LIZZY.	**JACK.**
MR. KEY!	Just say yes.

LIZZY. I will not have dinner with you on this porch or any porch!

JACK. *(Climbing back up the ladder.)* Resistance is futile.

>   *(Beat.)*

LIZZY. *Resistance…is futile?*

JACK. I said it.

LIZZY. I suppose you consider yourself quite the ladies' man.

JACK. Nope.

LIZZY. What then?

JACK. *Observant?*

>   *(Beat.)*

LIZZY. That sounds creepy.

>   *(LIZZY crosses to her yard and hastily begins removing laundry from the clothesline.)*

JACK. It is the best ginger beer you will ever have. And, I cook, by the way. Rib-eye, sweet purple hull peas, roasted sweet potatoes.

LIZZY. I don't eat red meat.

JACK. Is that / true?

LIZZY. I'M CUTTIN' BACK! I'm cutting waaaaay back.

JACK. I'm sure I can think of something you'll be interested in.

>   *(Beat.)*

LIZZY. Is that sex talk?

JACK. What?

LIZZY. Is it?!

JACK. It's just a damn porch date, Lizzy.

LIZZY. A *date?*

JACK. No, no, no. Not a date, just a whatever.

LIZZY. Oh. Just a *whatever.*

>   *(**LIZZY** grabs her basket and turns to exit.)*

JACK. *(Calling.)* You can bring your laundry.

LIZZY. *(Exiting.)* Oh, soooooo romantic, folding boxer shorts in the moonlight. Lucky girl!

>   *(**LIZZY** exits into her house, inadvertently leaving her beautiful white nightgown as the only thing hanging on the line. **JACK** stares at the nightgown.)*

JACK. *(Calling.)* I can help you outta some of your clothes too.

>   *(Long pause.)*
>
>   *(**LIZZY** re-enters with a tape measure.)*

LIZZY. *(Incredulous.)* What did you say?

JACK. *(Backpedaling.)* I said I can help you out. With some of your clothes…too.

>   *(**LIZZY** glares at him suspiciously and then snappily opens her tape measure.)*

Whatcha got there?

LIZZY. Measurin'. For a fence.

>   *(**LIZZY** begins to measure her yard.)*

JACK. A fence…

LIZ. Good fences, good neighbors.

(She thrusts one end of the tape measure at **JACK** *to hold.)*

JACK. Oh…a *mending wall.*

LIZZY. Robert Frost. Impressive.

JACK. I'm not a complete cretin.

LIZZY. You said it!

JACK. I can save you the trouble. This here's about twenty feet.

LIZZY. How do you know that?

JACK. *(Reading the tape measure.)* Minus two inches.

LIZZY. Ugh. Math genius.

JACK. I'm all pine and you're orchard, is that it?

LIZZY. You can stop quotin' now!

*(***LIZZY*** snatches the tape measure out of his hands.)*

JACK. Just what exactly are you tryin' to wall in, I wonder?

(She glares at him.)

LIZZY. *(Slow and deliberate.)* I would advise you to move your Maytag dryer off of the porch and into your perfectly good laundry room by eight a.m. Monday morning.

(She turns to exit and comes face to face with her nightgown that is still hanging on the line. She yanks it off the line and exits hastily.)

JACK. *(Calling.)* Lizzy…

LIZZY. *(Screen door slamming.)* NO!!

*(***JACK*** returns to his porch. He plugs in the Christmas lights and smiles, pleased with his handiwork. He returns the ladder to the side of the house. He notices one bulb out. He flicks it gently with his finger. It lights. He smiles, glances back at Lizzy's house, and then exits into his house.)*

(Lights fade.)

Scene 1.5

(Three weeks later. A few days before Christmas.)

*(**LIZZY** emerges from her house with a small wreath and a box of Christmas decorations. She opens the box and pulls out one of her favorite decorations, a bobblehead snowman family. She puts each family member on the porch cupboard, one by one – dad, mom, snow boy – and watches them dance. She returns to the box and discovers two Christmas stockings (hers and Jesse's). She stands there a moment, frozen, then hastily folds them back up and returns them to the box. She finds a Christmas ribbon and some wire for her wreath and begins assembling it. **JACK** emerges from his house, carrying a bag of trash. He wears an ugly Christmas sweater and a pair of festive reindeer antlers. He walks around to the side of his house to put the trash in the trashcan.)*

LIZZY. *(Calling.)* Mr. Key. How are you?

JACK. Lizzy.

LIZZY. *(Calling.)* You see anybody around my porch this morning?

　　(Beat.)

(Knowingly. Sweetly playful, half-distracted with the decorating.) It is the strangest thing...I had left a big pile of clippings off to the side there and when I came out just now, I noticed it was all cleaned up.

　　(Beat.)

JACK. *(Playing along.)* That's crazy...

LIZZY. *(Noticing his sweater for the first time.)* It is...

JACK. *(Walking toward Lizzy's porch.)* Blue ribbon, three years running, faculty Christmas party. And I am countin' Biloxi.

LIZZY. *(Highly amused.)* It's so good...I can barely talk about it.

JACK. *(Taking a bow.)* Thank you so much.

LIZZY. Oh, you're welcome.

>   (*Beat.*)

>   What can I get you, Mr. Key?

JACK. I'm just about to drive up to Clanton to visit my sister 'n them. You got any plans for Christmas?

LIZZY. I haven't decided.

JACK. You got family here?

LIZZY. No. Just my brother's family, but they're all in Savannah. Jesse and I used to ride up there, but I just can't do it by myself, it's too far. I might go in the summer though, my niece is gettin' married.

JACK. Can't be alone on Christmas.

LIZZY. I have invitations, Mr. Key. Jennifer Tate.

JACK. Oh?

LIZZY. Mmm hmm. Dr. Yancy and his wife…they're having an open house.

JACK. Well, that's good.

LIZZY. Yeah…

JACK. You could come with me if you like.

LIZZY. (*Smiling politely.*) Oh, thank you.

JACK. I mean it. She's got plenty of room. Think on it.

LIZZY. I saw you cleaned up some.

JACK. I did.

LIZZY. Thank you.

JACK. Did you hear the Hartmans are moving?

LIZZY. I did. Bobby got a job up in Birmingham.

JACK. He's a nice fella.

LIZZY. He really is. He asked me out once, years ago.

JACK. Oh?

LIZZY. Back when I was a sex goddess.

JACK. What?

LIZZY. He asked me / out once…

JACK. Back when you were a sex goddess?

LIZZY. Yeah.

JACK. I don't follow.

LIZZY. Oh, I don't think I need to elaborate on the ways in which the female body turns on its host, Mr. Key, I just had my dinner. Scissors, please.

>   (**JACK** *searches for scissors.*)

JACK. There is not a thing wrong with you.

LIZZY. You're just being polite, that's what Southern boys do.

>   (**LIZZY** *holds out the ribbon for* **JACK** *to cut.*)

JACK. (*Cutting the ribbon.*) What has poisoned your head this way?

>   (**LIZZY** *hands him the finished wreath.*)

LIZZY. (*A request for him to hang the wreath.*) Do you mind?

>   (**JACK** *walks to the door to hang the wreath for her. She watches him intently. Throughout the remainder of the scene,* **LIZZY** *sits on the porch stoop, tidying up an unruly box of ribbon while* **JACK** *fiddles with the wreath.*)

JACK. Can I ask a personal question? You don't have to answer it.

LIZZY. Alright...

JACK. Do you feel beautiful?

LIZZY. (*Regarding the wreath.*) A little higher...

JACK. I'm asking you as a friend. That's all.

LIZZY. What do you mean?

JACK. Well, you've been alone for a little while now, right? And I'm an outsider...I don't know your history, Lizzy. All I know is the woman I see right now and I have some opinions on her, if you're interested.

LIZZY. And what do you see?

JACK. You really want to know?

LIZZY. No.

>   (*Beat.*)

I can't believe how warm it is, can you? We had snow once, a few years back.

JACK. Oh, yeah?

LIZZY. Christmas miracle.

JACK. Never seen that on the Gulf.

LIZZY. No, I guess you wouldn't, that far south.

> (*Beat.*)

Did you love your wife, Mr. Key?

> (**JACK** *finishes with the wreath and leans against the porch railing.*)

JACK. I did.

LIZZY. Was she beautiful?

JACK. Beyond…

LIZZY. What did she look like?

JACK. She was…curvy…a little thing, enormous green eyes…crazy red hair that was just…impossible.

> (**JACK** *pulls a photo out of his wallet, hands it to* **LIZZY**.)

LIZZY. Impossible.

JACK. She always wanted the straight hair, but I loved how hers was just *everywhere*. Even toward the end.

LIZZY. Cancer…

JACK. She didn't want the chemo. And I don't think it would have – I mean I think it would have given her a few more weeks, but…

LIZZY. What was her name?

JACK. Amy.

LIZZY. Amy. How long has it been?

JACK. Two years.

LIZZY. And you miss her?

> (*Beat.*)

Of course you do. Do you believe that God makes mistakes, Mr. Key? It's something I secretly think about.

Maybe the things that happen to us and to the people we love are sometimes so awful and senseless, that we look for a reason...or someone to blame. But if there is a divine plan, how can we know what that is? I don't think it makes you any less godly if you believe he gets it wrong from time to time...do you?

> (**LIZZY** *hands* **JACK** *the photograph. He returns it to his wallet.*)

Jesse fell off a roof in Opelika. He died instantly.

JACK. You don't talk about him.

LIZZY. *(Realizing.)* No...

JACK. No.

LIZZY. *(Noticing the wreath.)* Can you turn it so the ribbon is at the top? I like the ribbon at the top...

> (**JACK** *adjusts the wreath.*)

Why did you move away from Biloxi, Mr. Key?

JACK. *(Stalling.)* What's that?

LIZZY. Why are you here? You're here for a reason.

JACK. This job came up. / Seemed like a good –

LIZZY. That's not the reason.

> *(Beat.)*

JACK. Too many reminders.

> *(Beat.)*

LIZZY. I finally gave away the last of Jesse's things over the weekend. Still a few boxes in the attic, but I know what you mean, though. At least I think I do. I asked Jesse to fix this porch step a few days before he died. He said "Put it on the list."

> *(Beat.)*

Would you like to change the subject?

> (**JACK** *smiles appreciatively.*)

How's school? Is my room still free?

JACK. I straightened everything up. Put some plants in there.

LIZZY. You did?

JACK. I go in there sometimes, when I need the quiet.

LIZZY. I like imagining that.

JACK. It's not quite as sexy as it sounds. Bologna sandwich.

LIZZY. *(Amused.)* Do you want to know what I love about a school Mr. Key?

JACK. What's that?

LIZZY. I'll give you a hint. It's not the quiet. The noise, Mr. Key, the *noise*. Like a war zone…just…filling up every hallway…every classroom. Always with the *me, me, me*! That constant hum of hundreds of teenagers all talking at the top of their lungs, everything is of the utmost importance, obviously!

JACK. Life or death…

LIZZY. Oh, life or death!! Squeaking tennis shoes and lockers slamming shut! Man, it feels so good to slam a locker!

JACK. It does!

LIZZY. Doesn't it?!

JACK. It sure does.

LIZZY. I remember when I was that age, it seemed like there was always some boy to slam a locker for. Slam it so hard and then give him that look – you know, the *look* – and flip my hair and just walk away with my algebra textbook, like *take that* shit-for-brains!

JACK. *(Amused.)* You kept the boys running.

LIZZY. Oh, I did.

JACK. I bet you had to beat 'em off with the stick.

LIZZY. Oh, no, the boys in my school were different, Mr. Key. They wanted me for my big giant brain, hordes and hordes: *Lizzy, meet me in the library…fiction.*

JACK. That's fiction, alright.

LIZZY. Well, except for Jim Godwin. He wanted me for my brain…among other things. In fact, he gave me a promise ring my junior year. But then he went and got a football scholarship to Georgia Tech.

(Beat.)

LIZZY. And that was the end of Jim Godwin.

JACK. Jim Godwin chose poorly.

LIZZY. Oh, yeah?

JACK. Georgia Tech?

LIZZY. Smart-ass!

(Beat.)

JACK. *(Regarding the wreath.)* Hey. Is it perfect?

*(**LIZZY** stands and turns to look back at the house.)*

LIZZY. It is.

(Beat.)

JACK. Well…if I don't see ya…

*(**LIZZY** hugs him. He is touched by the gesture, awkward as it is.)*

(Blushing. Hugging her back.)

Okay…

*(**JACK** turns to exit but then returns with the reindeer antlers and puts them on **LIZZY**'s head. She curtsies in her new crown of horns.)*

(Beat.)

LIZZY. Merry Christmas, Mr. Key.

JACK. Merry Christmas, Lizzy.

*(**JACK** exits. **LIZZY** watches him leave. Her smile dissolves.)*

LIZZY. *(Suddenly very aware of her own solitude.)* Happy New Year…

*(**LIZZY** gathers her supplies and exits into the house.)*

(Lights fade.)

Scene 1.6

(Four months later. Spring. Late evening. The sound of distant thunder.)

(JACK stumbles sleepily out onto his porch, barefoot in pajamas. He carries his pillow and a blanket.)

JACK. *(Yelling back at the house.)* There is no such thing as ghosts!!

> *(JACK unfolds a cot and makes his bed on the porch.)*

It's the plaster and the stupid roof. And that's all it is, so shut up!

> *(Angrily making his "bed.")*

A widower in a widower's house. How do you like that?

> *(Punching his pillow.)*

Stupid.

> *(JACK slowly drifts off to sleep. LIZZY, wearing a robe and drinking a glass of wine, walks out onto her porch to check on the approaching thunderstorm. She sees JACK on his porch...)*

LIZZY. *(Calling.)* You know there's a storm coming, Mr. Key, you ought not to...

> *(She notices him sleeping. She walks over to his yard and studies him a moment. She sees the dryer at the edge of the porch. She walks over to it. She reaches her hand out to touch it, and as her fingers touch the metal, the dryer buzzes, loudly.)*
>
> *(Recoiling in horror.)*

Shiiiiiit!! I'm 'on have a heart attack!

> *(LIZZY takes a moment to collect herself. She looks over at JACK, who stirs, but does not waken.)*
>
> *(A whisper.)*

Mr. Key?

(LIZZY takes a swig of her wine and sits down beside him on the porch. JACK snores softly. LIZZY talks in the safety of knowing he can't hear any of it.)

LIZZY. I went by the school today. Looks like I'll be starting back after the summer. Ooooh, they had so many questions. Don't worry. I protected your reputation.

(Sound of distant rolling thunder.)

Bob Searcy asked me out for coffee. I declined. I guess that's one good thing about being a grieving widow, you can just…blame it on death. He said I have nice legs…for a Baptist. I baked him a casserole. It seemed like the appropriate response.

(Beat.)

I don't remember the last time I was on any kind of a date. Before Jesse, I mean. Okay, I won't lie. I do remember. Six years ago, July third, over on Tybee Island in Savannah. My brother's wedding. There was a groomsman…*Michael.* We danced at the wedding, snuck out, went over to the beach and watched the sun go down. Talked and talked. He told me he had big plans to open his own hardware business, and I told him he could do it too and he believed me. And then there was the *not talking.* It was like falling…falling and falling over and over. Like we'd always have that moment, and I could just die right then and there, because nothing else mattered.

(More thunder, storm approaching.)

In the morning we went over to the coffee shop and got breakfast. Walked out onto the pier…fed the seagulls. He pulled me into him and I put my head on his chest and he said…*I will never forget you.*

(A whisper.)

I will never forget you…

(Beat.)

And then he kissed me and left for California. I knew we'd keep in touch, I just knew it. But he…he told me his life was complicated, some girl back home. And he never made me any promises, so I told myself I had no right to feel anything. I still do that, by the way. Real *fun* game I play with myself. But you know, I wonder sometimes, if there was a way of wiping that memory away, would I do it? I don't know what's worse…to have a moment like that and lose it…or to go through life in the dark…

> *(Bright flash of light followed by a loud thunder clap. The chimes tinkle softly in the wind.* **JACK** *shifts his weight on the cot. Suddenly aware of* **JACK**'s *presence,* **LIZZY** *tucks him in, stands, and walks toward her house, sipping her wine.* **JACK** *opens his eyes [unseen by* **LIZZY**]. *It is evident he's heard all of it.)*

One thing I do know. I don't trust any of it. Not anymore. Because walks on the beach at twilight…they don't mean anything. It seems as if they must, but they don't.

> *(***LIZZY** *climbs her steps, her foot landing on the creaking porch board. She presses it with the ball of her foot a few times.)*

I really need to fix that step…

> *(The storm is upon them now. Everything is alive and churning. Lightning flashes and thunder chases in hot pursuit.)*
>
> *(The rain is sheeting now, like a river from the sky. The chimes and bottles dance and sing as* **LIZZY** *reaches her hand out to catch the droplets.)*
>
> *(***JACK** *watches the entire spectacle from his porch.* **LIZZY** *steps out into the storm. She closes her eyes and lifts her face to welcome the deluge.)*
>
> *(Lights fade.)*

End of Act I

ACT II

Scene 2.1

(Three months later. End of summer. Twilight.)

(Jack's yard is now clean and tidy. Festive garden lights hang from the porch and there is a makeshift table set for dinner in front of a charming vintage porch glider that now sits in his yard.)

*(**LIZZY** approaches from around the side of her house, keys in hand, carrying her purse and wearing sunglasses. She stops in her tracks to see **JACK** fussing over the table setting and wearing an apron that reads "Will Grill for Kisses.")*

LIZZY. *(Astonished. Tickled to death.)* Oh, my gosh – OH… MY GOSH!

>*(Taking in every detail.)*

What are you – what on earth?!

>*(Regarding the glider.)*

Ha! Would you look at – THAT is the cutest thing I've ever seen!

>*(Looking at the porch and the garden lights.)*

This is, I just can't – this is AMAZING! Is this –

>*(Suddenly noticing the table set for two.)*

Oh.

>*(Beat.)*

Oh, I'm sorry…

JACK. Lizzy.

LIZZY. You have a date.

JACK. Welcome back.

LIZZY. *(Only slightly jealous.)* Well, Mr. Key. She must be somethin'. It looks good out here!

> *(**LIZZY** notices an item missing from the setup.)*

Candles?

JACK. Oh!

LIZZY. Not the tall ones, no.

JACK. Okay.

LIZZY. You have some?

JACK. Umm…I have some / of the…

LIZZY. Citronella? Votives?

JACK. Yeah.

LIZZY. That's fine. Just a few, ya know? Then it won't be so buggy.

> *(Beat.)*

Thank you for looking after the house, Mr. Key.

JACK. I got your mail. It's…just inside there. Kitchen counter.

LIZZY. Oh, thank you. I'm so glad the heat has lifted.

> *(Awkward pause.)*

JACK. You look good.

> *(Beat.)*

LIZZY. So do you.

JACK. How was Savannah?

LIZZY. Oh, I got my hair done for the wedding, remind me to show you the pictures. I looked like the Bride of Frankenstein.

> *(Trance-like.)*

It was lovely though. There's just something about a wedding, ya know?

> *(Beat.)*

Well. I'll leave you to it.

>(**LIZZY** *turns to exit.*)

JACK. Lizzy…

LIZZY. Hmm?

JACK. *(Nervously.)* I know this is our *last hurrah* with school startin' on Monday, so…I was kinda hoping you'd come over and try my cooking.

>*(Beat.)*

LIZZY. Oh.

JACK. I mean, unless…

LIZZY. No.

JACK. Or just a drink, maybe. Glass of wine.

LIZZY. No, I – I'm sorry, I just assumed you had a date…

>(**LIZZY** *flushes, suddenly realizing she is the intended date.*)

That's…umm…okay. Sure. Can I, uh / …can I –

JACK. Whenever.

LIZZY. Okay. Okay.

>(**LIZZY** *turns to exit, but then spins back around to give him a gift.*)

Oh, I brought you something.

JACK. Oh?

>*(She freezes, thinking better of it.)*

LIZZY. *(Very flustered now.)* I'll bring it. I'll bring it…

>*(Beat.)*

Just a little something.

>*(He smiles.* **LIZZY** *turns to exit.)*
>
>*(Now at her porch door.)*

This is so awkward.

JACK. *(Highly amused.)* Yeah.

>(**LIZZY** *exits.*)

(A montage:)

*(**JACK** fusses with a few things on the table and then exits into his house for candles, as...)*

*(**LIZZY** emerges as if in her private dressing area, holding up an outfit to an invisible mirror. She sighs at the reflection. Exits, as...)*

*(**JACK** re-enters with some votive candles and two wine glasses. He attempts to light a votive with a torch lighter. The lighter refuses to light. He exits for another lighter, as...)*

*(**LIZZY** re-enters her dressing area, all dressed, and stands before the mirror. She adjusts her bra strap, fidgets with her outfit, and then exits, as...)*

*(**JACK** re-enters with some wine and fills two glasses. He attempts to light one of the candles with a different lighter, but again, the lighter will not light. Exits as...)*

*(**LIZZY** re-enters her dressing area and puts on some lip gloss. **JACK** re-enters with a little vase of flowers and sets it on the table. He reaches into his apron pocket for a book of matches.)*

*(**LIZZY** exits, as...)*

*(**JACK** strikes a match and finally lights the two votives. He removes his apron, sits on the glider, takes a swig of wine, and looks nervously at Lizzy's house, as...)*

(Lights fade.)

*(Lights up on **LIZZY** and **JACK** sitting on the glider, finishing up the last bites of red beans and rice.)*

LIZZY. No, look, I'm not kidding.

*(**LIZZY** pulls out her cell phone to show him pictures.)*

I said you gotta fix it so it won't blow around, I want it down, but like barrettes, or whatever, and she said,

"Honestly if you want my opinion…that just looks like two pigtails hangin' down." Look, she had these tattoos and they were scary, from prison maybe. Pair of scissors on one arm – look, there's my hair! SO AWFUL! She said, "Honey, I know aaaaalll about beach hair, we gotta be teasing that crown to Jesus." Look there it is from the back! You could hang pots from it!

> (*She turns to see* **JACK** *smiling at her.*)

What?

JACK. Nothin'.

LIZZY. Somethin'…

JACK. You just…seem different.

LIZZY. I do? How?

JACK. I've never seen you this happy.

LIZZY. (*A realization.*) I am happy.

JACK. It looks good on you.

> (**JACK** *tidies up the dishes.*)

LIZZY. You're a good cook, Mr. Key. I'll let you do that more often.

JACK. You want some ice cream? I made some.

LIZZY. You did not make ice cream!

JACK. (*Almost a threat.*) Oh, I made it.

LIZZY. Stop it.

JACK. Butter pecan.

LIZZY. Noooooo, that's my poison!

> (**JACK** *turns to exit for ice cream.*)

No, let's wait, I need to settle.

> (**JACK** *sits back down.*)

(*Shaking her head at him.*) Ice cream.

> (*Admitting she might have underestimated him.*)

Hmm.

> (**LIZZY** *returns to looking at wedding pictures on her phone.*)

LIZZY. They went on their honeymoon to Antigua. Did you have a honeymoon, Mr. Key?

JACK. We went to Disney.

LIZZY. No, really?

JACK. It was a blast.

LIZZY. Gosh, that sounds fun. Small World? Little tea cups?

JACK. Yep. What about you?

LIZZY. Well…I wanted to go see some shows on Broadway and he wanted the mountains. I cried on my honeymoon.

JACK. Oh…

LIZZY. It was awful.

> *(Beat.)*

I've been goin' through Mr. McElway's letters. So personal. It seems he and Miss Minnie had a falling out about ten years ago. And I don't know what happened, they ended up in separate rooms, I guess. I had no idea they were goin' through all that. I mean, I'd like to believe if an *entire* world was collapsing all around me, I'd have taken some notice.

> *(Beat.)*

And those letters…the ones written in chicken scratch. Those were his too. Written around the time he broke his hand during a fight they had in the kitchen.

JACK. *(A whistle.)* Pfeeewww…

LIZZY. He loved her.

JACK. How do you know?

LIZZY. *(Handing **JACK** a letter.)* This is one of the recent ones.

JACK. You opened it?

LIZZY. Find some quiet time.

> *(Beat.)*
>
> *(**LIZZY** begins to speak, but stops herself.)*

JACK. What?

LIZZY. I never loved my husband. Is that shocking?
JACK. Did he love you?
LIZZY. Yes, he did.
JACK. Why did you marry him?
LIZZY. Because he's a good – because he was…a good man.
JACK. I've heard good things.
LIZZY. Oh?
JACK. Salt of the earth. Loyal.
LIZZY. Yes. God-fearing. Good to his workers. He was. He was all those things. And he was good to me.
JACK. And do you miss him?

>   *(She looks at* **JACK** *intently.)*

LIZZY. I never told anybody that before, Mr. Key…the part about me not loving my husband.
JACK. You can tell me anything.
LIZZY. I'm rather a private person.

>   *(Beat.)*

I don't know how people don't know, I mean, they must, I didn't cry at the funeral.
JACK. People deal with grief in different ways. Would you like some more wine? Something stronger?
LIZZY. *(Playfully suspicious.)* Whatchoo got?

>   *(***JACK** *pulls out a small bottle of moonshine.)*

Ooooh…is that from down yonder, Yellowfoot Road?!
JACK. What do you know about Yellowfoot Road?
LIZZY. Ooooh, you got that apple pie shine!
JACK. Quick, like a band-aid.

>   *(***LIZZY** *drinks.)*

LIZZY. Owww!! Dammit all!

>   *(Chasing it with a swig of wine.)*

Liquid fire, SHIT!

>   *(Off his amused reaction.)*

LIZZY. Well, there's no water!

> (**JACK** *drinks.* **LIZZY** *leans back in the porch glider and looks up at the night sky.*)

Is this the part where we get all wasted and loose-lipped and slip dangerously into uncharted territory?

JACK. *(Looking at the stars.)* Let's do *that*.

> *(The dryer buzzes.)*

LIZZY. I'm a terrible drinker. There's all this liquor in the house, I have no idea what any of it is, the bottles are so pretty, I dust them. It always looks so delicious when people are sipping cocktails on TV, you know, the soap operas? We had a girls' night over here last year and Missy Odom showed me some recipes, but I might have been gone by that point, I can't remember any of it.

JACK. I drive people to it.

LIZZY. To drink?

JACK. Yeah.

LIZZY. Oh, lord, I'm sure I do.

JACK. I drink whiskey now and then. When I'm grading papers.

LIZZY. Yeah?

JACK. Keeps me honest.

> *(Beat.)*

I leave comments.

LIZZY. *(Amused.)* What? Bad?

JACK. Rivers of blood.

> (**JACK** *goes to unload the dryer.*)

Hey, who's your most disappointing student?

LIZZY. *(Thinking.)* My most – oh gosh…umm…Willie Morgan.

JACK. *Willie Morgan?*

LIZZY. Yeah.

JACK. He's a straight-A student.

LIZZY. Psh. Maybe *I'm* the disappointment.

JACK. How?

LIZZY. Oh, that child. Every year in the spring, I ask my kids to write a personal essay, you know, something autobiographical. And he writes, he does.

JACK. Oh, I've seen it.

LIZZY. He's good, he's got it. And so, they all came in with their stories…and you know, all over the map, but it's good, it's a good project. And you know most of the boys will write about football or huntin', what else is there, / south Alabama…

JACK. Right.

LIZZY. …And I never really expect anything else. So a few of 'em got up to read, aloud, you know, in class, and then I called on Willie to read his. And he looked at me…and he said he hadn't written anything.

(Beat.)

"Oh really, Mr. Morgan? You don't have anything for me today?" "No ma'am." Few hours later, I found his paper…torn up in the trash.

(Beat.)

Mr. Key, I can't even tell you, it was so beautiful. He had written about a hike on the Appalachian Trail, with words…I hadn't ever seen in that order. And by a sixteen-year-old boy? I mean I was speechless. I've not seen a boy write like that in my classroom, ever. The girls do. They get it, but you know, that's all they do is bleed all over the page, they're so expressive, and everything so devastating, ya know, but the boys…

JACK. We don't want to seem foolish.

LIZZY. What *is* that?

JACK. Play it cool. Learn guitar.

LIZZY. See, that is so short-sighted. And only a high school girl would put up with that shit. A woman wants a man who can *spell.* Or write a love note or know the ones to steal.

(Beat.)

LIZZY. Where was I? Oh, yeah, okay, so the next day I took him out into the hallway and I asked what happened. And he said he had forgotten the assignment. And I said now that's not true and you know it. And he asked me how I knew and I showed him the papers…

(Beat.)

He just looked at me. And I said, now Willie, what is it, what are you afraid of? And it was like one of those scenes from a tragic movie. The bell rang and all the kids rushed out into the hall…but we were sorta frozen there for a minute like in slow motion and he had these tears in his eyes. I reached out to him and he gave me the saddest look and just walked off.

JACK. Poor kid.

LIZZY. Broke my heart.

(Beat.)

"The stars lay on the ragged ridge line…and blankets of cotton mist. A white stag in silhouette, blackened by the light."

JACK.	**LIZZY**.
(A whisper.) Pfffff…	Sixteen years old.

JACK. Wow.

*(**LIZZY** notices a sock that has fallen out of the basket. She goes to pick it up and searches the laundry basket for its mate.)*

LIZZY. I've read it a hundred times, I still have it. He just pushes it all down so no one can see it. And I wonder maybe…if his mama hadn't died when he was little…or if he'd had a daddy who understood his potential…if maybe he'd have the courage for it. And then I think… no. Because then what would he have to write about? Other than his perfect life. And no one wants to read that.

*(**LIZZY** is now busily pairing all the socks together.)*

JACK. *(Charmed.)* Lizzy.

LIZZY. *(Holding up a shirt.)* Okay, this is cute. I hadn't ever seen you wear this one.

> *(**JACK** fills their wine glasses.)*

JACK. It occurred to me this morning, we have something to celebrate.

LIZZY. Oh?

JACK. Today's our one-year anniversary.

LIZZY. What?

JACK. I moved in one year ago today.

LIZZY. A year?

JACK. Yep.

LIZZY. It seems like way longer.

JACK. Doesn't it?

LIZZY. Oh well. We're in it now.

> *(They toast.)*
>
> *(Tossing him the shirt.)*

I like this one. Wear it more.

> *(**LIZZY** notices the whites and colors all mixed together in the basket.)*

Well, you have just mixed it all up here, huh, tossed salad.

> *(She moves the basket closer to the glider.)*

Ooh, I'm feelin' a little wobbly, Mr. Key, you gettin' tipsy?

> *(He smiles in response. She begins folding the clothes.)*

Mr. Key?

JACK. Hmm?

LIZZY. How come you never had kids?

JACK. We wanted to. We were trying to, actually.

LIZZY. Oh, I'm sorry.

> *(Beat.)*

Maybe they're in your future…

JACK. I hadn't ruled it out. What about you?

(She answers by throwing him a pair of his boxer shorts.)

JACK. Too personal.

LIZZY. We're the leftovers, Mr. Key. Ever thinka that? People say all the time that life isn't fair...but have you ever noticed they never say that about death? No matter how bad it is, death just gets a free pass.

JACK. How do you mean?

LIZZY. Well, like if someone's been suffering for a long time and finally passes, they say well death is a mercy. But if someone dies of an accident all of a sudden, you know, with no warning, they just say...life's not fair. I mean I do think it's true, life's not fair, but neither is death, and I think death kinda sucks, personally, if you ask me. There's no fairness to it.

*(**LIZZY** wrestles with a sheet. **JACK** stands to help her. Throughout the following exchange, they fold the sheet together.)*

JACK. They tell you to remember the good times...but that's not how it works. You can't edit out the end, like it didn't happen.

LIZZY. No, I guess not...

JACK. The end is the loudest part. I've seen death come around, barge right in. Make itself at home. Seen it take my whole world, everything I loved, take it right out of my arms. But that's alright. Cuz I know I was lucky. I got to say goodbye. I got to walk her through it. I got to bathe her...comb her hair...read to her from all those...*ridiculous* magazines.

*(**JACK** takes the sheet from **LIZZY** and smooths it down, tenderly tucking it into the basket and pressing it lightly with the palm of his hand.)*

And finally...when the time came...I got to be brave for both of us and smile at her and see her smile back at me...and give me permission...

LIZZY. *Permission.*

JACK. You know, Lizzy…for a long time I made death out to be this monster because it wouldn't *fucking* leave. Even when it was done with her, it just…*hung around* for months and months…ate all my food.

LIZZY. *(Trance-like.)* But you're not bitter…

(Tipsy and stumbling.)

My husband cheated on me. Isn't life just the craziest? You pray and pray to God on your hands and knees for deliverance from your own awful existence, from your own sickening self and to take it all away and then one day, God answers all your prayers, like magic. Whoosh!

(Childlike.)

All gone!

JACK. Lizzy…

LIZZY. Oh, I almost forgot!

*(**LIZZY** crosses to her porch.)*

I was at the big folk art festival up in Savannah last weekend and I got you this precious little Catholic church bird house!

*(**LIZZY** holds up the bird house, calling from across the yard.)*

Do you love it?!

JACK. I do…

LIZZY. It's good, right?

*(**JACK** crosses to Lizzy's porch.)*

JACK. It is.

LIZZY. Oh, but it needs a little something…

*(She hands the bird house to **JACK** while she attempts to attach a bow. She falters.)*

JACK. Lizzy…

LIZZY. *(Childlike.)* I got you a bird house…

JACK. Hey…

(Long pause.)

LIZZY. His mama knew it was all a lie. All she wanted was a grandbaby. I just couldn't do it. God, the way she would look at me. I've never seen such hate in my life.

JACK. Come and sit down.

LIZZY. I know what you see. You don't have to tell me. You can save yourself the trouble. Here's your bird house.

*(**LIZZY** walks over to Jack's yard and looks for a place to hang the bird house.)*

You can hang it next to the Virgin Mary on your porch and she can – she can go in there when it gets cold at night.

(Laughing at the absurdity of it.)

Who am I kidding? She can't fit inside a bird house...

*(**LIZZY** falters. She collapses on the glider. She holds onto the bird house.)*

JACK. Lizzy...

(Silence.)

LIZZY. I was the one who gave him permission.

JACK. *Permission.*

LIZZY. To cheat.

JACK. What?

LIZZY. I know, right?

(Beat.)

He would reach for me. And I...couldn't. I just – it's not that I'm afraid of that. You think I'm afraid of sex, Mr. Key?

JACK. Lizzy...

LIZZY. I'm not! I'm not! Sex is good, Mr. Key. I mean, *good* sex is good, right?

JACK. Yeah.

LIZZY. I'm not afraid of it.

(A whisper.)

I – I miss it.

JACK. Has it been a while?
LIZZY. *(As if to say "you have no idea.")* Oh…
   (Beat.)
   I wanted it, Mr. Key. Just not with him.
   (Beat.)
JACK. Was there someone else?
LIZZY. No. There never was. I was faithful. I was a good wife. He gave me something solid, something real. I didn't want a divorce. I don't believe in it. And so I sat him down one night and I told him if he needed that…if he needed to go and find that somewhere else, I wouldn't stop him. And it was awful. He was so angry. He started yelling at me, said it was a crime against God what I was doing. I said, but I can't give you what I don't have, I can't feel what I don't feel. I said, what do you want me to do, just lay there and lie to you? He threw his plate across the kitchen. We didn't talk for weeks. When summer came around, I noticed he was working longer hours, coming home late. And then one night I heard him leave the bed around midnight. And I knew he was – I smelled his cologne. I didn't say a word, but in my head I was like…yes. *Go. Go do…what you need to do.* He came back a few hours later like nothing had happened…he put his hand on my shoulder, like he always does, but I laid real still…waited for him to fall asleep. And then I went downstairs and sat at the kitchen table for a while…watched the sun come up. Cooked him some eggs and he came down and we sat there and ate. Total silence. And then when he stood up to go to work he kissed me on my forehead and said, "I love you." And I looked up at him…and all the color just drained right out of his face…the sadness of a *million days* of him knowing I'd resent him for it, but it wasn't that at all, I just didn't want it floatin' around in my head, ya know? And that's what I wanted to tell him, but I didn't say it, I didn't say *anything*. And then he went off to work down to that roofing job in Opelika

and I sat there at the table…fell asleep, I guess, I don't know how long I slept, I woke up to a phone call from Mr. Ledbetter: "Jesse took a fall."

(A realization.)

I've ruined lives Mr. Key.

JACK. No.

LIZZY. Yes, I have. I know how to love, I do. I just didn't know how to love him. He is a good man. He is *such*…a good man. And now, I feel like I'm surrounded by all these people, all over town – *(Mimicking.) I'm so sorry.* I'm going to Hell for the things I've done.

JACK. You're not going to Hell.

LIZZY.	**JACK.**
I am. I know I am.	No, no Lizzy, you're not.

LIZZY. How do you know?

JACK. Because I know!

LIZZY. You don't! I've destroyed lives, Mr. Key. / Whole lives!

JACK. No.

LIZZY. Yes, I have! He was my best friend! I could have given him his whole life back, and I hung on / like a damn IDIOT!

JACK. You're so wrong.

LIZZY. How?

JACK. It wasn't your choice to make, Lizzy! It was his. Don't you see that? You wanna feel bad because you stayed? Because you stuck around and tried to do right by the man?

LIZZY. Oh, you just know it all, don't you? You know everything. You have it all so carefully arranged. Sleeping in the yard. And your laundry outside because you're too afraid to go in there and take back your damn life! And you won't kiss Daphne for the same reasons. You…are afraid. You're afraid you might *actually* feel something. Or that you'll keep losing…the people that you love.

(Beat.)

The only ghost in that house…is you. And it's too bad, isn't it? Because you have a mortgage. And now we're neighbors. And one of us has to MOVE. Because I don't want to be your neighbor anymore!

> (**LIZZY** *grabs* **JACK** *and kisses him hard on the mouth, clawing at him.*)

JACK. Lizzy. Lizzy…

> (**JACK** *relents for a moment, but then pushes* **LIZZY** *back, holding onto her wrists.*)

LIZZY. *(Suddenly horrified, disoriented.)* Oh no…

JACK. Shhh shh / shhhhh…

LIZZY. No. No. No, no, no, no. You have become too familiar!

JACK.	LIZZY.
Lizzy! Don't go like this… hold on…	Let me go. Let me go, LET ME GO!!

> (**LIZZY** *pulls away from* **JACK** *and shoves him. Hard.*)

LIZZY. YOU STAY AWAY FROM ME!

> (**LIZZY** *exits into her house.*)

JACK. *(Chasing after her.)* Is that how it is, Lizzy? I'm not feeling bad enough for you? Or feeling it in the right order? I got news for you.

> *(Pounding on the door frame.)*

It's a fucking nightmare! And there is no end! There's no structure. It doesn't give a SHIT about you. Or what you're doing, or whether you're happy, or whether it's convenient…or anything at all about your cute little plans!!

> *(Staggering backward.)*

It just lays there, waiting…like a crazy ex-girlfriend. With a shotgun.

> (**LIZZY** *appears in the doorway.*)

You don't know my life.

LIZZY. I hate you.

*(**LIZZY** disappears into the house.)*

*(**JACK** stands there frozen. Stunned. He staggers to his own yard and somehow steps on a nail along the way. There are yelps of pain, and it's all he can do to stifle a stream of expletives, but he manages to do it. He hobbles to the glider and looks at his foot. He tries to remove the nail, but it is stuck good, and he realizes he is not in the right mental or physical state to deal with it. He opens the jar of moonshine, looks at the candles in disgust, pours moonshine on them to extinguish them, and then takes a giant swig.)*

JACK. Perfect.

(He drinks.)

(Lights fade.)

Scene 2.2

*(Later that evening. Out of the darkness, a flashlight clicks "on." Fairly drunk now, **JACK** lies on the porch glider singing an old drinking song* and making spooky flashlight faces in the dark, clicking the flashlight on and off.)*

JACK. *(Elvis-like.)* Thank you!

*(**JACK** puts the flashlight to his forehead.)*

Shutthefuckupshutthefuckupshutthefuckupshutthefuckup.

*(**JACK** notices the letter still on the table. He sits up, opens it, and reads it by the glow of the flashlight.)*

"Miss Minnie Faye. I'm 'on put this letter with the others, you know the place. I'm bettin' you don't want to hear from me, but this house is worse than awful since you went away. I feel sorry for the sad bastard that ends up with this dump. And I'll be so glad to die and get out from under it."

*(Opposite side of the stage: a pool of light on **LIZZY** – soliloquy style – who addresses the audience as if speaking directly to Jesse as **JACK** silently reads along...)*

LIZZY. *(To Jesse.)* "Big tree limb fell on the roof over the summer...and there was a leak in the hallway all through July. Went up there to fix it...still ain't right. I do not understand about the plaster. Seems like no

---

*A license to produce *Maytag Virgin* does not include a performance license for any songs under copyright. If the licensee wishes to use a copyrighted song, the publisher and author suggest that the licensee contact ASCAP or BMI to ascertain the music publisher and contact such music publisher to license or acquire permission for performance of the song. If a license or permission is unattainable for that song, the licensee may not use the song in *Maytag Virgin* but may create an original composition in a similar style or use a similar song in the public domain. For further information, please see Music Use Note on page iii.

matter what I do, the mix comes out wrong. And you know I'm too cheap to call a professional. But that's alright. Go ahead and tell me you told me so."

(JACK *reads aloud, mostly to Amy now...*)

JACK. "I miss the smell of your cooking."

(*They read aloud...*)

BOTH. "All the times I wished for you to leave me, and now you went and done it."

(*He reads.*)

JACK. (*To Amy.*) "They brought you to me in a little box. I have no idea what I'm supposed to do with you now. If I could tell you some things..."

(*She reads.*)

LIZZY. (*To Jesse.*) "If I'd known you'd be taken so quick...I'd want you to know how grateful I am for you puttin' up with my sorry ass...sticking with me as long as you did. For making us a home...and for keeping me safe... from myself. The truth is, I did love you. And I still do."

(*Lights out on* LIZZY. *She exits.*)

(JACK *cradles the letter and the flashlight. He slowly falls to pieces on the glider.*)

(*Lights fade.*)

Scene 2.3

(The next morning. **LIZZY** *emerges onto her porch with a cup of coffee. She sees* **JACK** *asleep on the glider. She pulls her cell phone out of her pocket and dials his number. Jack's phone rings. He awakens, confused, searching for the noise. He pulls his cell phone out of his pocket and sees Lizzy's number on the caller ID. He looks over at Lizzy's porch to see her standing there, then answers but does not speak. Over the following exchange, they sometimes talk directly to each other and sometimes into their phones.)*

LIZZY. I'm calling you on the phone. It is Lizzy. The basket case. From next door.

(Calling across the yard.)

I can hear you breathin'.

(Into the phone.)

Did I wake you?

*(***JACK*** shakes his head "no.")*

Okay, good. Cuz I've made a list. Hold on.

*(***LIZZY*** takes a few hits from her coffee and pulls out a notepad from her pocket.)*

Okay, I'm / back.

JACK. I miss her. Some days I miss her so much, I wanna curl up and die. I was dead in Biloxi. As dead as a man can be without actually dying. When she finally passed, there wasn't anything left for me to do, except…float around all day. House started closin' in, I couldn't breathe. Get in my Jeep and just drive and drive. Check into motels, sleep at the school. Folks at St. Bernard would pray for me, I said don't do it.

LIZZY. You asked 'em not to?

JACK. I said pray for Nacine Waters, her kid's run off, or Randy Sawgrass, his baby's got cancer…

LIZZY.	JACK.
Mr. Key…	Don't pray for me, I'm good, I'm a healthy man. I thought I was.

(Silence.)

(JACK looks across the yard at LIZZY.)

JACK. You kissed me.

LIZZY. That wasn't me.

(Beat.)

JACK. *(Calling across the yard.)* It's a good thing I'm not your type!

LIZZY. Mmm hmm.

JACK. *(Calling.)* Can you imagine?

(Beat.)

LIZZY. Please don't wait around for me, okay? I mean it. *Call Daphne.* Besides, I can't fall in love with a Catholic.

JACK. And why not?

LIZZY. It's just not done.

JACK. We're cannibals you know. The rumor's true.

LIZZY. Oh, yeah, y'all eat Protestant babies, right?

JACK. Mmm hmm. Boiled. Like Lobster.

LIZZY. Hey, did I ever tell you about the time I snuck into my uncle's Episcopal church down in Eufala and ate up all the communion wafers?

JACK. Whoa! Man, you must have really wanted the body of Christ!

LIZZY. I never did find any wine, but I did look around when I was trying on all the vestments. *Ves-ta-ments?* Vestments…

JACK. *(Instructing.)* Vestments.

LIZZY. *Vestments.*

(Beat.)

I really am sorry.

JACK. Stop.

LIZZY. So many unknowns, Mr. Key. We're just supposed to jump in the water, I guess. With the sharks.

JACK. Maybe that's it.

>	*(Beat.)*

LIZZY. Am I a good kisser?

JACK. Compared to what?

>	*(Beat.)*

LIZZY. I'm going back to bed.

JACK. Lizzy.

LIZZY. ?

JACK. I need you.

LIZZY. ??

JACK. I'm really sorry to do this to you, but there's something in my foot.

>	*(**LIZZY** goes to inspect.)*

LIZZY. In your foot?!

JACK. A nail, maybe. Something awful.

LIZZY. How do you know it's awful?

JACK. Because when I tried to remove it, it was awful.

>	*(**LIZZY** exits for supplies – a hand towel, a bowl of sudsy water, and a first-aid kit.)*

LIZZY. And you've just been sitting here festering and catching tetanus all night long, how wonderful!

JACK. That's 'cause I'm smart.

LIZZY. *(From offstage.)* You could knock on my door, ya know!

JACK. *(To himself.)* That's 'cause I'm smart.

LIZZY. *(From offstage.)* Well, there's no blood.

JACK. No blood?

LIZZY. *(From offstage.)* Not yet.

JACK. What is it?

LIZZY. *(From offstage.)* Splinter!

JACK. What?

LIZZY. *(From offstage.)* Hang on.

JACK. A splinter?

LIZZY. *(From offstage.)* Does it hurt?

JACK. Yeah.

LIZZY. *(From offstage.)* We'll get you fixed up.

JACK. You ready for school tomorrow?

LIZZY. *(From offstage.)* Mr. Key, I'd like to enjoy my last day of freedom.

>*(JACK limps toward LIZZY's porch.)*

JACK. Like tending to an old man's foot. *(More to himself.)* There is much to be enjoyed by that.

LIZZY. *(From offstage.)* Seen worse. Done worse.

JACK. Well, I certainly do appreciate it.

LIZZY. *(From offstage.)* We have 1,440 remaining unadulterated minutes, this will take five. *(Emerging from the house.)* Ten if you're lucky. *(Holding out a bottle of aspirin to JACK.)* Come put your foot where I can see it.

JACK. *(Regarding the aspirin.)* I don't need it…

LIZZY. They're for me!

>*(JACK opens the bottle for LIZZY.)*

JACK. I can drive us in tomorrow, if you like.

LIZZY. Fine, long as I can pick the music.

>*(LIZZY swallows the pills down without water and continues right on with her work.)*

(Regarding the "nail.") You want me to take it out?

JACK. *(Regarding the pills.)* I have never seen a girl do that.

LIZZY. You never met me.

>*(LIZZY yanks the "nail" out of JACK's foot. JACK folds over in pain.)*

JACK. DAMN, WOMAN!!

LIZZY. Breathe!

JACK.	LIZZY.
I –	Nope! Just breathe! CCR, John Lee Hooker, Def Leppard, quick, name some going into battle songs!

JACK. Eye of the Tiger!

LIZZY. *Nice!* Good one.

>   *(**LIZZY** applies pressure to the wound. She rinses off the object that was stuck in Jack's foot and holds it up for him to see.)*

Ooh, you caught a big one. What is that, a wood screw?

JACK. You said it was a splinter!

LIZZY. OH MY GOD THERE'S A TRAIN COMING – see how scary that sounds?

JACK. Oh, you're gon' get it.

LIZZY. You're gonna need a tetanus shot.

>   *(He nods.)*

Soon. You promise?

>   *(He nods. **LIZZY** presses a washcloth against the wound and gives it to him to hold.)*

Hold that.

>   *(Throughout the following, **LIZZY** disinfects the wound and washes his entire foot with warm, soapy water.)*

Did you read the letter?

JACK. That was rough.

LIZZY. Can you imagine writing a letter like that to someone you know is never going to read it?

JACK. No. But I can see why he needed to write it.

LIZZY. Why do we stick with somebody for so long even after it's tragic and awful? Is it fear?

>   *(Beat.)*

What are you afraid of Mr. Key?

JACK. *(Picking one from thin air.)* Clowns?

>*(Beat.)*

What a question. Uh…let's see. Well, I suppose when I was younger, I was afraid I'd never amount to anything. And then much later, obviously, I was afraid I might lose it all. Which, of course…I did. After that, what is there to be afraid of really?

>*(Beat.)*

Dying alone?

LIZZY. What about living alone?

JACK. Oh, I've gotten real good at that. Ya know, when you think about it, there's really only two reasons to be afraid of something…either it's gon' kill you…or you're gon' kill it.

>*(Beat.)*

LIZZY. You mean like being chased by a bear?

JACK.	**LIZZY.**
Umm…	What is your favorite way to die? If you could pick, I mean. Have you thought about it?

JACK. Quick.

LIZZY. Quick how?

JACK. Bullet to the head.

LIZZY. Whoa. Really?

JACK. Yeah.

LIZZY. So violent!

JACK. What about you?

LIZZY. *(Digging through the first-aid kit.)* Well, probably in my sleep but if I can't have that, I'd like to be trampled by an elephant.

>*(Beat.)*

JACK. How is that *not* violent?

LIZZY. Oh, it's violent. Does it still hurt?

JACK. Little.

LIZZY. Okay. Little's better than nothing, if it was nothing, we'd need to amputate.

JACK. Pffffff.

LIZZY. Relax!

JACK. Yeah.

> *(Pause.)*

LIZZY. This is nice. Lookin' after somebody…

> *(**LIZZY** applies a band-aid and finishes up with his foot.)*

Don't forget the tetanus.

> *(Beat.)*

You got a nail in the other foot?

> *(Beat.)*

LIZZY. Lemme see…

> *(They exchange a playful look. **JACK** gives her his other foot.)*

How do your feet get so filthy?

JACK. *(Playfully. As if to ask, "What are you up to?")* I work at it.

> *(Silence.)*

> *(**LIZZY** washes the other foot. Her touch is overwhelming to **JACK**. He closes his eyes.)*

LIZZY. Are you in pain, Mr. Key?

> *(**JACK** opens his eyes and searches her face.)*

Are you?

JACK. *(Softly.)* No…

> *(She flushes.)*

LIZZY. You have nice feet, Mr. Key.

> *(As **LIZZY** leans toward the basin of water, her breast presses against **JACK**'s foot. He notices.)*

LIZZY. Thank you for this morning. Sometimes I forget I'm allowed to be happy. Miss Minnie Faye could have left him, she could have found somebody better. Well, maybe not *better*, but...better for *her*, ya know? But she stayed. Is that what a good heart does, it just breaks and breaks until it's good at being broken? What *is* that? Didn't she want to be happy?

JACK. Have you ever heard the term *horse latitudes*?

LIZZY. Is that a song by The Doors?

(He nods, amused that she gets the reference.)

JACK. It's also a place.

LIZZY. Horse latitudes...

JACK. Somewhere in the subtropics, I think. But it's *calm* there. All the time. There's not a lot of rain or storms or anything really to speak of, just a lot of sunshine.

LIZZY. Sounds perfect.

JACK. It does. It does. Except...there's a story – apocryphal, probably – but, so the story goes that back in the trade days when the Spanish would cross the Atlantic in these massive sailboats, ya know, carrying the food and livestock to the colonies...sometimes, when they reached...*horse latitudes*...the ships would just stall...in the ocean. No wind, just...just the stillness of nothing.

LIZZY. *Stillness of nothing...*

JACK. They might be stuck there for weeks, for months... running out of food and water. And the wind might pick up and they would be on their way but then sometimes, the wind never came...and the rations were gettin' thin and the animals began to starve. And so the crew had to make a decision...on what to do about the horses. And if it got bad – *bad enough* – they would bring the horses up on deck – the dead ones or the sick and the dying – and they would umm...send 'em off the boat.

LIZZY. Into the ocean?

(Beat.)

While they were still alive?

JACK. Sometimes.

LIZZY. Oh…

> (**LIZZY** *dries his foot and holds it in her warm hands.*)

JACK. Like I said, it's probably a made-up story. But, still beautiful.

> (*Looking intently at her.*)

Survival.

> (**LIZZY** *looks at him quizzically, not understanding his meaning.*)
>
> (*Clarifying.*)

Do you…*remember*…the pain?

LIZZY. What pain?

JACK. The pain that was there…*before.*

LIZZY. What – oh…

> (*Silence.*)
>
> (**LIZZY** *thinks for a moment, recalling the pain of her marriage. It all comes rushing back – the longing, the heartache…the guilt. She looks up at* **JACK.**)

LIZZY. Yeah…

JACK. *(Pointedly.)* Good.

> (*Beat.*)

LIZZY. *(Heartfelt.)* Thank you.

JACK. It's all you, Lizzy.

> (**JACK** *looks down at Lizzy's textbooks.*)

You're gonna be back in the pit tomorrow.

LIZZY. Did you kiss Daphne?

JACK. *(A million meanings.)* A year's a long time…

> (**LIZZY** *presses her hand firmly against* **JACK***'s leg so that there is no misunderstanding. She asks again…*)

LIZZY. *(Pointedly.)* Did you?

> *(Silence.)*

> *(***JACK*** *looks up at* ***LIZZY*** *and leans his head back against the porch railing. He takes in the whole of her, the fullness of the moment. They stare at each other intently.)*

JACK. Now why would I go and do a thing like that?

> *(***LIZZY*** *stares back at him, absorbing the full weight of his meaning.)*

> *(Lights fade.)*

Scene 2.4

(Later that evening. Two a.m.)

(**JACK** *emerges from his house with an urgency, headed toward Lizzy's house, but everything seems to be standing in his way. He reaches for the t-shirt in his laundry basket – the one that she favored from the night before – but is distracted by the new bird house Lizzy left on his porch. He exchanges his wind chime with the new bird house. He descends his steps only to turn around and change his shirt. He descends his steps yet again, only to turn around and retrieve the wind chime, which he then hangs on Lizzy's porch. He takes a step back to gather his courage. He then ascends her stairs and knocks on the door.*)

(He descends her stairs to wait for an answer. No answer.)

(He ascends her stairs and knocks again, louder this time, then returns to the bottom of the steps to wait. A porch light is turned on. **LIZZY** *peeks through the door…)*

LIZZY. What is it?!

JACK. Come on out.

LIZZY. Oh my gosh, what?

JACK. Just come out.

LIZZY. Are you okay? Is it your foot?

JACK. I'm fine.

LIZZY. You're fine, it's two in the morning, is something on fire?

JACK. There's no fire Lizzy, I mean there is a fire –

LIZZY.	**JACK**.
What?	Just – just come out!

LIZZY. *(Not amused.)* Well, what do you want, you crazy boy?

JACK. I want you. I want you right now, that's what I want.

LIZZY. What?!

JACK. Come out on the porch, Lizzy.

LIZZY. What? No!

JACK. Lizzy.

LIZZY. Why?

JACK. Because it's *necessary*.

LIZZY. For what?

JACK. *(At the end of his rope.)* Could ya come out?! Would ya do that?!

> *(Beat.)*

LIZZY. Hold on…

> *(She turns to get a robe.)*

JACK. No! No, I will not hold on. I'm done holding on. Let me see you.

LIZZY. I'm in my nightgown.

JACK. Lizzy!

LIZZY. Can I get a robe first?

JACK. No. No! You cannot get a robe. Stay just like that, don't change a thing, just *walk out here*.

LIZZY. I cannot believe you right now!

JACK. Lizzy. Listen to me. It's just you and me. It's two a.m. It's quiet. Everyone's asleep. And I have been so, so patient. Please…

> *(Beat.)*

Let me *see* you.

> *(**LIZZY** finally realizes his intentions. She hesitates. She opens the door and walks out onto the porch. She is barefoot, and she wears a long, white nightgown that glows in the moonlight. There is sleep in her eyes, and she squints from the porch light. Her unruly hair falls down around her shoulders. She nervously crosses her arms to cover her body.)*

Don't.

(LIZZY puts her hands down and leans against the railing. JACK looks over her entire body. He is transfixed.)

(A whisper.)

Turn around…

LIZZY. Turn around?

JACK. Please.

(LIZZY hesitates for a moment. She slowly turns around. JACK inhales and exhales sharply. She turns back around.)

LIZZY. Making me nervous…

(JACK takes a few steps toward her. She stands slightly above him on the porch step. He reaches up to touch her shoulder, tracing down her arm and hand to the tips of her fingers. He slowly traces down the folds of her long, white nightgown. LIZZY begins to shake. She closes her eyes, overcome with emotion. She reaches her hand out to touch his hair.)

JACK. My god…

LIZZY.	**JACK**.
I can't do this.	Beautiful…
No…	Shhhh…
I'm not…	Lizzy. You are. And I don't mind saying that I wouldn't mind saying that every night for a long, *long* time.

LIZZY. *(A whisper.)* You are crazy.

JACK. Yeah…

(JACK reaches his hand out to help her down the stairs. They are face to face.)

LIZZY. *(Barely breathing.)* I told my pastor I was having impure thoughts about a Maytag dryer. He said there was no such thing. I said but it has a heated steam cycle, and he said, "Ooooh, there might be something to that."

>   *(Beat.)*

You smell like Joe Namath.

JACK. *(Amused.)* What?

LIZZY. *(Shaking.)* I always think of him from those Brut commercials. And when I smell a man that smells good, I always think he might smell like Joe Namath. And then I imagine him in that other commercial with the pantyhose and I get all confused.

JACK. Old Spice.

LIZZY. Old Spice?

JACK. Yeah.

LIZZY. *(Playing it off.)* It's good.

JACK. You know, Joe Namath was a Catholic.

LIZZY. *(Voice cracking.)* Oh?

JACK. Mmm hmm.

LIZZY. We have many fine Catholics all over this town, they're not bad people, just misguided.

JACK. You're still a sex goddess.

LIZZY. See what I mean –

>   (**JACK***'s kiss is so lethal, it nearly flattens her.* **LIZZY** *emerges for air, breathless.)*

Well…we'll need to work on the kissing.

>   *(Inaudible. Unseen by* **JACK***.)*

OH MY GOD!

JACK. I've been waitin' a whole year to do that.

LIZZY. *(Bleary-eyed drunk.)* Was it good for you? Jack?

JACK. *(Teasing.)* Oh, we're all on first names now.

LIZZY. *(Blushing.)* Shut up…

JACK. Lizzy, I'm in love with you.

>   *(Beat.)*

LIZZY. *(Retreating up the steps.)* You are smoking-high-stoned-out-of-your-mind-drunk, what you saying, what are the words you are saying –

| **JACK.** | **LIZZY.** |
| I'm not drunk, Lizzy. | You are not in lov– how can you be in love with me? |

JACK. Are you blind?!

LIZZY. No. I'm not…

JACK. Well?

> *(Beat.)*

LIZZY. *(A realization.)* I didn't want to see it.

JACK. I figured.

LIZZY. I'm so awful.

JACK. Yeah, you are.

LIZZY. I'm sorry.

JACK. That's not a turn off for me, Lizzy. When you dig in I just want more of you.

LIZZY. You do not.

JACK. I love everything about you. Even the things you think I won't. You don't scare me.

LIZZY. *(A joke.)* Well, shit.

> *(Beat.)*

I don't know how to do this.

JACK. Good!

LIZZY. No, I mean it, I think I forgot some things.

JACK. Tell me you don't want me. Tell me.

> *(Beat.)*

LIZZY. I do want you.

> *(Beat.)*

Is that shocking?

JACK. I already knew.

LIZZY. You don't know *anything*.

JACK. Mmm hmm. It's all in my head.

LIZZY. *(Babbling.)* Oh, you are so hilarious, ya know that, with / your "observations."

JACK. You can't hide from me Lizzy, I see it all.

LIZZY. What do you see?

JACK. You wanna know?

> *(Beat.)*

LIZZY. Nope.

JACK. I watch you when you don't know I'm watching. You're left-handed. Your gardening gloves don't match. You wear lavender, but sometimes, on special days – and I haven't figured out the pattern – you wear another fragrance…

LIZZY. Gardenia.

JACK. *Gardenia.* You collect wind chimes in low registers… and baby elephants. You take walks, but you wait for the light. You listen to Sinatra in the kitchen and Coltrane in the bedroom.

> *(LIZZY glares at him.)*

Stop me any time…

LIZZY. What else do you know?

JACK. I know that I want you. *All of you.*

LIZZY. All of me?

> *(Beat.)*

That's a lot.

JACK. I am aware.

> *(Long pause.)*

LIZZY. You have a Maytag dryer on your porch. It's been out there a year. And I have to ask myself why it doesn't bother me anymore, it hasn't bothered me for a while, actually.

> *(Beat.)*

Mr. Key, can I tell you something?

JACK. *(Correcting.)* Jack.

LIZZY. Jack. *(Beat.)* I don't remember anything about being happy. I don't know if I've ever been happy. And I'm standing here, and I'm wanting to trust you. I'm wanting to tell you that you are a really good kisser. And that I have *feelings* for you. *Important* ones. And that as terrified as I am right now, I really do want more of those kisses. And I'm saying all of this – *out loud* – while being fully and completely aware that you might run away.

JACK. I have a mortgage.

LIZZY. No, no, NO! I am not imagining this, Mr. Key! This is very real, the fears that I have are very, *very* real. Every single time I have reached out for something like this it has fallen right through my fingers. And I have to think that maybe some people just aren't meant to have the things they want in this world, ya know, or to be loved in the way that they ought to. I don't want to believe that that's true, but *dammit*, what / else is there?

JACK. Lizzy…

LIZZY. I am alone, Mr. Key. And I always have been. And I'm so tired. I am so tired of waiting…and why – why does a man just stand there and let a woman ramble / on and on like this!

JACK. Ask me how I know.

>   *(Beat.)*

Just ask me…say… *How do you know, Jack?*

>   *(Long pause.)*

LIZZY. "How do you know…Jack?"

JACK. Because the only thing I'm afraid of, Lizzy – the only thing that scares me anymore – is that I won't ever be as good in life…as I am when I'm with you.

LIZZY. Who *are* you? *(Looking around the yard.)* Did you really just say that to me?

JACK. *(Amused.)* What are you looking for?

LIZZY. A hidden camera, are you serious? What are you, from the future?

JACK. *(Enamored. Taken.)* I love you.

> *(**LIZZY** inhales sharply.)*
>
> *(Silence.)*
>
> *(She stares at **JACK**, unable to speak.)*

Take a walk with me.

LIZZY. A walk?

JACK. Yes.

LIZZY. Where?

JACK. *(Emotional.)* I don't care.

LIZZY. This is a school night.

JACK. Mmm hmm.

LIZZY. You're crazy.

> *(**LIZZY** concedes. She looks around her porch and finds an afghan and wraps it around her shoulders.)*

JACK. Oh, good, a blanket.

LIZZY. *(Resisting the implication.)* No!

> *(She puts on a pair of gardening clogs.)*

We have two perfectly good homes right here, this is the shit teenagers do.

> *(Beat.)*

I look like a mental patient.

JACK. *(Referring to her ensemble.)* So hot.

> *(Silence.*
>
> *They stand. Apart. Together.*
>
> *Every memory…every daydream…every emotion – in distinct succession – picked up and returned by the other, like a silent game of tennis:*
>
> *The longing. The panic. The fear.*
>
> *The knowing. The fight. The release.*
>
> *Last night. Last year. Last chances.*

> *The lost. The found. The new.*
> *Forever. Tomorrow. Right now.*
> *The scars. The salve. The rain.)*

Lizzy…

LIZZY. Why aren't you kissing me?

> (**JACK** *reaches for her hand.*
> *He guides her down the steps.*
> *He brushes back her hair.*
> *He cradles her face in his hands.*
> *He envelopes her lips with his own.*
> *Exhale…*
> *Lights fade.)*

End of Play